Tonight was differe...

Instead of guilt, Asher was coming ho... Tess. She'd dropped everything to come watc... Cameron.

This was the first time they were alone. The perfect opportunity to tell her about Cameron. "Don't go. We haven't talked since I got back."

"I don't have much to say…"

"Do you ever think about us? Ever wonder what might've happened if we'd married like we'd planned?"

"We would've been kids struggling to raise a baby and go to school."

"But we would've been together." He searched her face.

"It wouldn't have been enough."

"How do you know?" He moved closer. "You were everything I needed. I would've done whatever it took so we could be a family."

Uncertainty filled her eyes and she hesitated. For one second he clung to hope.

Till she shook her head and ran out the door. "I can't do this."

There's something I have to tell you… The words hovered on his lips. Tonight wasn't the time to reveal his secret.

Would it ever be?

Heidi McCahan is a Pacific Northwest girl at heart, but now resides in North Carolina with her husband and three boys. When she isn't writing inspirational romance novels, Heidi can usually be found reading a book, enjoying a cup of coffee and avoiding the laundry pile. She's also a huge fan of dark chocolate and her adorable goldendoodle, Finn. She enjoys connecting with readers, so please visit her website, heidimccahan.com.

Books by Heidi McCahan

Love Inspired

Home to Hearts Bay

An Alaskan Secret

The Firefighter's Twins
Their Baby Blessing
An Unexpected Arrangement
The Bull Rider's Fresh Start

Visit the Author Profile page at LoveInspired.com.

An Alaskan Secret

Heidi McCahan

LOVE INSPIRED
INSPIRATIONAL ROMANCE

LOVE INSPIRED®
INSPIRATIONAL ROMANCE

Recycling programs for this product may not exist in your area.

ISBN-13: 978-1-335-75920-7

An Alaskan Secret

This edition published by arrangement with Harlequin Books S.A.

For questions and comments about the quality of this book, please contact us at CustomerService@Harlequin.com.

Love Inspired
22 Adelaide St. West, 41st Floor
Toronto, Ontario M5H 4E3, Canada
www.LoveInspired.com

Printed in U.S.A.

For thou, Lord, art good, and ready to forgive;
and plenteous in mercy unto all them
that call upon thee.
—*Psalm* 86:5

To my sweet friend Kristen.
Thank you for helping me with the details.
I couldn't have written this one without you.

Chapter One

A disconcerting prickle at the back of Tess Madden's neck had replaced her usual giddy anticipation. The beginning of a new school year had never made her this anxious. She couldn't identify the source of her unease, though.

And the not knowing why was about to drive her bananas.

Tomorrow marked the start of her second year teaching her own classroom full of second-graders. Her first back in Hearts Bay, Alaska. After earning her bachelor's and master's degrees at the university in Fairbanks, it thrilled her to be back in her hometown on Orca Island.

Well, mostly thrilled. Unless a smell or a glimpse of a certain landmark triggered a painful memory, rocketing her back in time to the summer that changed everything. Those moments happened more often than she'd expected since she'd moved back two weeks ago. Still, she'd chosen to come home. Chosen to accept this teaching position with the added responsibility of working as a reading specialist. Chosen to be back with her sisters and her parents, who were all still grieving her brother's tragic death.

So why the ominous sensation prowling around like a hungry grizzly bear stalking its prey?

She sidestepped the temptation to allow overthinking to immobilize her. Setting up a classroom for fifteen second-graders shouldn't be this difficult. And her training and certification more than qualified her to tackle the challenge of helping children improve their literacy.

Relax. You've done this before.

She'd wanted to be a teacher ever since she'd been a kindergartener in this same building almost twenty years ago. From day one, she'd adored everything about life in the classroom. Learning new things filled her with joy. And once she learned to read, exploring the world through the pages of a book became her favorite pastime. She never complained about practicing her penmanship once her teacher handed her a notebook and a freshly sharpened pencil.

Clutching her insulated coffee mug between her hands, Tess turned in a slow circle. Clean desks organized in five pods of three sat waiting. She'd already printed her name in neat letters on the whiteboard at the front of the spacious classroom and posted the daily schedule with her new assortment of dry-erase markers. Every cubby along the wall had a label with a student's name and their corresponding number. What was she forgetting?

The clock on the wall inched closer to 4:30 p.m. Time to get going. She'd planned to meet her sisters for dinner at the café and had hoped to squeeze in a quick workout first. Maybe her classroom wouldn't feel completely ready until her students arrived in the morning. Or maybe she held herself to an impossibly high standard because she wanted to impress her new coworkers.

Teaching in the same building where she'd been a student added a whole new level of anxiety. Most of the women who had taught her still worked here. The principal had changed, but the front-office staff hadn't. In some people's eyes she was still that girl who got pregnant, then left the island after she placed her baby with his adoptive family. She'd become a Christian a few years ago at a Bible study for college students. Her friend had encouraged her to memorize the verses about being forgiven, but sometimes shame clung to her like the pungent odor of rotting fish.

The familiar hollow ache settled in her chest. Ever since her brother, Charlie, had died in a commercial fishing accident last summer, she'd tried to blame that ache on her grief over losing him. Except now she realized that sensation also reminded her of the baby that no longer belonged to her.

He was probably getting ready to start school this week, too. Did he have a new backpack and a lunch box he couldn't wait to show his friends? Did his parents help him get new clothes and sneakers that fit?

Stop.

She turned around, as if finding another task to complete might assuage the regret and the longing for her child.

The books. That's right. How could she forget?

She hadn't unpacked her own personal library of age-appropriate books yet. Her students would love the reading nook in the corner by the window, filled with two denim-covered beanbags and a lamp on a side table.

A couple of posters she'd hung on the wall celebrated reading as a vehicle to see the world. Growing up on an island, kids needed to know that there was a great big wide world out there.

She crossed the room, set her coffee down on the windowsill and flipped open the latches on the plastic bin containing her books. The previous teacher had left behind an incredible bookshelf with plenty of space to display the books face out so the kids could see the titles and the pictures on the cover. Tess's portable speaker streamed a popular song from her phone's playlist. She danced along to the beat while she pulled her books from the bin and placed them lovingly on the shelves.

"Knock, knock." Someone rapped on the doorjamb of her open classroom door.

Tess shrieked and dropped a paperback copy of *Toys Go Out* on the gray carpet. She glanced over her shoulder. "Mrs. Franklin, you scared me to death."

"I'm sorry, dear." Mrs. Franklin glided into the room. "I stopped by to say hi. Didn't mean to scare you."

Tess picked up the book, tucked it into the shelf, then quickly moved to her desk and paused the song on her phone. "Thanks for stopping by. Are you all set for tomorrow?"

"As ready as I'll ever be." Mrs. Franklin thrust her hands in the pockets of her ever-present cardigan sweater and smiled sweetly. She still wore her blond hair styled in bouncy round curls and looked almost exactly as Tess remembered her. Did the woman stay perpetually fifty-five? Sure, her hair had more silver than blond now, and her sweet face carried a few more lines, but that wide smile and those kind blue eyes hadn't changed a bit.

"You probably don't even have to think twice about the first day of school anymore. You're such a pro at this."

Mrs. Franklin offered a good-natured wave of her hand. "I don't know about that. Even after thirty years of teaching, there are always a few surprises, especially on the first day."

"Oh, don't say that," Tess groaned, pressing her palm to her chest. "I'm already so nervous."

"Don't be." Mrs. Franklin surveyed the room. "Everything looks great. I'm sure you're a fantastic teacher. Our test scores last year were not what we'd hoped so we're delighted to have a reading specialist. Besides, it's been a long time since there's been a Madden in this building."

"Thank you. That's sweet of you to say."

Tess had always admired Mrs. Franklin and it was an honor to teach across the hall from her unofficial mentor.

"Speaking of surprises and Maddens." Mrs. Franklin leaned against the nearest desk. "I had a new student come by with his dad today and he reminded me so much of your brother."

The comment landed like an ice pick poking her sharp and fierce. Tess clutched the edges of her desk with her fingers. "Really?"

"It's the strangest thing. The child is the spitting image of his father, but there was something about the little guy that reminded me of Charlie at that age. It's probably the mischievous gleam in his eye or the high energy level. He bounced around my room like a rubber ball. He's going to keep things interesting this year."

Tess forced herself to draw a deep breath into her constricted lungs. She and her sisters had always wondered if Charlie had fathered any children. He'd been a wild one, always flirting but never staying in a committed relationship. Except Mrs. Franklin's story made little sense if this new student resembled someone else. "Who—who is it? The boy and his dad?"

Mrs. Franklin's expression pinched. As if she'd suddenly realized what she'd said. "Oh, you know him, too. It's Asher Hale and his son, Cameron."

Wait. *What?* Tess's legs wobbled and she fell back into her chair. Asher had moved to Oregon. She'd checked, double-checked and surfed through many a social media post just to be sure. How could he be here? And how could he possibly have a *son*?

Asher Hale had a list of reasons a mile long justifying his decision to move back to his hometown.

And only one significant reason he shouldn't.

This tight-knit community tucked into a secluded bay on an island off the Alaskan coast held a complicated past. One he wasn't quite ready to confront.

"Can we have cheeseburgers for dinner?" Cameron bounced beside him like a kid on a trampoline, oblivious to the debate warring inside Asher's head. "Except no cheese. I only want ketchup. Plus fries. Lots and lots of fries."

"We'll see." Asher opened the front door of his childhood home, then stepped inside, still gripping the doorknob as Cameron darted around him. The sweet aroma of cookies baking greeted them.

"Grammie, we're back!" Cameron hollered, his wet sneakers squeaking against the tile entryway floor as he raced into the house.

"Cam, use your inside voice, please." Asher closed

the door. That boy had one speed. Fast. Unless he was asleep, which wouldn't be for another four hours. Potentially sooner if Asher used the early-to-bed-because-school-starts-tomorrow argument.

He'd been doing far more negotiating than he was comfortable with lately. Ever since they'd moved from Oregon back to his hometown of Hearts Bay on Orca Island in Alaska, he and Cameron had struggled to find their usual easygoing groove. Sure, this was the first time he'd ever cared for Cameron on his own. Did every single parent wrestle with these challenges when they went through a major life change? He mentally filed that thought away for later when he had a minute to text his older sister, Krista, for advice.

"Daddy, Grammie is eating raw cookie dough." Cameron's triumphant declaration drew a groan from Asher. He moved into the living room, where he found Cameron beside the glass coffee table, pointing at his grandmother.

Under any other circumstances, this might make Asher laugh. Except his mother's guilty expression reminded him that these circumstances were far from normal. His father had left her after thirty-five years of marriage, and she'd responded like Asher knew she would: creating unnecessary drama everywhere she went. Worse, she aggravated him and his siblings by refusing to manage her diabetes. Another reason why he'd moved home. Somebody needed to keep an eye on Sharon Hale.

"Now, if you're going to tattle, then I guess that means I don't have to share." His mother frowned and pointed her spoon at Cameron. His expression crumpled and his brown eyes immediately filled with unshed tears.

"Mom." Asher infused as much disapproval as he could into that single syllable. Cameron's sorrow pulled Asher across the room. He sank to his knees and folded his young son into a hug.

Cameron hid his face against Asher's plaid buttondown shirt.

Asher had always considered himself a peacemaker. The diplomatic middle child of the Hale family. Never in a million years did he imagine a scenario where his seven-year-old tattled on his fifty-seven-year-old mother. He'd always been proud of his ability to defuse tension and help find a compromise. Something told him he'd met his match.

He rubbed Cameron's back and mouthed a warning toward his mother, nestled under a leopard-print blanket on the cream-colored sofa. *Be kind.*

She rolled her eyes, then set her spoon and contraband bowl of raw cookie dough on the glass coffee table.

"Oh, Cameron, you know Grammie is just teasing. You and your dad can have as many cookies as you want."

Cameron pulled away and heaved a pitiful sigh, his dark eyes finding Asher's. *Did she mean it?*

Asher stuffed down a harsh reprimand aimed at his mother. He'd tried to be super patient since she was still reeling from her divorce, which was final after the new year. But he and Cameron had moved back to Hearts Bay less than a week ago, and this was already the second time Mom had hurt Cameron's feelings. He'd have to speak with her privately about her thoughtless comments.

"Let's get a cookie, buddy." Asher guided him toward the kitchen. "Maybe we can find some milk— Oh, wow."

He stopped short in the doorway to the kitchen. Freshly baked chocolate chip cookies beckoned from the cooling rack beside the stove. But that was the only good thing in sight.

Dirty dishes, spilled flour and sugar, reusable tote bags filled with groceries plus remnants of his mother's baking session covered every flat surface.

"Whoa," Cameron whispered. "What happened?"

Asher scrubbed his hand over his face. "Looks like Grammie has been busy."

"Don't worry about the mess," Mom called out. "I'll clean up later."

"Disgusting." Cameron stepped around something sticky on the floor and reached for a cookie. "Want one, Daddy?"

"Hold on." Asher pointed toward the sink. "Wash your hands first, please."

A few minutes later, they'd washed and dried their hands, and found a clean plastic cup and some milk that hadn't expired. Asher helped Cameron carry a plate with two cookies into the living room.

Cameron set the milk carefully on a side table. He even remembered to use a coaster, and then flopped on the love seat opposite Asher's mother. Asher set the plate down, then grabbed the cookie dough bowl before his mother finished it.

"Hey, I'm not done." Her blue eyes flashed with irritation. "Who told you not to eat cookie dough, anyway?"

"Aunt Krista."

"Oh. Well. No big surprise there. She always was a bit of a party pooper."

Cameron's giggle rippled through the room.

"She's a pediatrician, Mom. I'm sure she knows what she's talking about."

Asher felt loyal to his sister. She and her husband had graciously allowed him and Cameron to live with them for the past seven years. She'd helped him when Cameron had been a fussy newborn, spent countless hours entertaining him while Asher studied so he could finish his degree in four years. He never would have survived being a single dad without Krista and her husband's support.

Which was why he bristled every time Mom took a cheap shot.

"Have you checked your blood sugar recently?"

She looked away, pointing her remote control at the flat-screen TV mounted above the fireplace. "I've been managing my diabetes all by myself for quite some time."

Asher leaned his elbows on his knees and clasped his hands together. "Then you don't need me to remind you that too much sugar isn't good for you."

Mom selected another episode of her favorite home renovation show, then dropped the remote onto the blanket spread across her lap. She wiggled her toes. "I still have both my feet and I'm not blind yet, so I'd say I'm doing fine. Thanks for your concern."

Her sarcastic tone grated. Asher clasped his hands tighter to keep from grabbing a throw pillow and screaming into it.

"I'll tell you what." Her eyes sparked with a mischievous gleam that made him nervous. "Let's grab dinner at Harbor Lights Café and I promise I'll be a good girl and eat lots of protein."

"Do they have cheeseburgers there?" Cameron mumbled around a mouthful of cookie.

Asher wanted to veto his mother's suggestion because agreeing felt like an endorsement of her less-than-stellar behavior. He'd bought groceries and had plenty of ingredients back at his place to fix a healthy dinner but letting someone else cook was too tempting to pass up. After a busy day running errands and visiting Cameron's new classroom, he wanted to take the path of least resistance between now and bedtime. Feeding him a burger and fries was much easier than arguing about three bites of green beans and grilled chicken.

"Fine," he conceded. "But I want to order takeout."

He was too worn-out to keep a tired boy occupied in a restaurant, even at a casual place like the café.

"Sounds good to me." His mother shrugged and reached for her phone. "You guys tell me what you want, and I'll call it in."

While Cameron repeated his request for a cheese-free burger and fries, Asher mulled his options. He didn't regret moving home. At least not yet. People with limited professional experience didn't usually get wildlife biologist positions on the island. He was blessed to have the job and excited to start work in two days. But his patience with his mother was already wearing thin. After he dropped Cameron off at school in the morning, he'd come by and have a frank discussion about her health and her snarky attitude.

"Why didn't you tell me that Asher Hale was back on the island?"

"Hello to you, too." Eliana slid onto the bench seat opposite Tess. "How was your day?"

Tess squeezed her eyes closed. *Breathe, just breathe.* When she opened her eyes, her sister had pulled her apron over her head, and sat facing her.

"I'm sorry. I didn't mean to sound rude," Tess said. "I just can't believe he's here."

The shocking news had eliminated her plans to work out. After Mrs. Franklin had dropped the truth bomb about Asher and his son, she'd pulled herself together and finished putting her books away. Then she'd locked up her classroom and driven straight to her sister's waterfront restaurant, Harbor Lights Café.

Eliana folded the apron and set it on the vinyl cushion beside her. The empathy reflected in her chocolate-brown eyes made Tess feel a tiny bit less guilty. "I love that you think I know everything that goes on in Hearts Bay, but I don't. If I'd heard that Asher Hale had moved back, you would've been the first to know."

"Thank you." Tess picked at the paper ring encircling her napkin and silverware. "It's stupid of me to freak out like this, especially after all this time, but I was so certain he'd moved out of state. I really didn't plan on seeing him again."

"Are you sure he's here?"

"Oh, he's here. Mrs. Franklin came into my classroom today and told me Asher had registered his son, Cameron, and the boy's going to be in her class."

Eliana gasped. "His son?"

"Yep." Tess pushed the silverware aside and pressed her icy palms to her fiery face. "How could he possibly have a seven-year-old?"

Eliana wrinkled her nose. "That would mean—"

"That means everything his mother said was true." Eliana reached across the table and squeezed Tess's forearm. "I'm so sorry. I've always liked Asher. It really annoys me that Sharon Hale thrives on being the center of attention, and she spread the juicy details of his personal life all over the island. It's almost like she's happy that his wife left him."

Tess winced. She had heard the story, too, even hundreds of miles away in her dorm room at the university in Fairbanks. She hadn't wanted to believe it, either. How had Asher met someone new and started a family so quickly? And was she supposed to feel sorry for him that the marriage hadn't lasted?

"I would've understood moving on, especially after we had such a traumatic breakup. But if he has a seven-year-old, then he obviously had a girlfriend while he was still with me." Emotion tightened her throat. The baby boy she'd given birth to in May of her freshman year of college had been placed with a family off the island in a closed adoption. Asher had opposed the adoption from the minute she'd shared her plan. They'd argued right until the day before her water broke. "He insisted that he wanted to start a family. Looks like he got his way."

The truth still hurt. Snippets of their heated conversations replayed in her head. He'd been persuasive. She'd wavered. Oh, how she'd wavered. Part of her wanted to believe that they could make it together, just the three of them, but she'd been so afraid their relationship wouldn't survive the stress of having a baby when they were both so young. After watching countless single parents struggle in their community, she hadn't wanted that for herself. Or for Asher. She'd chosen a better life for their baby, with two parents and a stable home, but lately she'd regretted her choice more than ever before.

Eliana glanced out the window overlooking the marina. "Mia and Rylee just pulled into the parking lot. We can order as soon as they get here."

"There's one more thing." Tess leaned closer. "Mrs. Franklin mentioned something that I wanted to share with you."

Eliana's dark brows sailed upward. "Tell me."

"She said that the little boy, Asher's boy—" She could barely say the words out loud. "She said he reminded her so much of Charlie."

Disbelief washed over Eliana's face. "Our Charlie?"

"Yeah, so weird. Right?"

"She probably should've kept that to herself." Eliana frowned and scooted over on the U-shaped bench seat to make room for their sisters.

The bell on the door jangled as Mia and Rylee rushed into the café.

"Sorry we're late." Mia unzipped her coat. "My last patient had to be admitted to the hospital." She pulled her ponytail holder loose and let her long auburn hair swish over her shoulders as she sat down.

"Oh no," Tess said. "I hope everything's okay."

Mia's smile didn't quite reach her eyes. "I think he'll be all right. It's been a day."

Tess sensed there was more going on than just a strenuous day at the clinic where Mia worked as a physician's assistant, but she didn't press for more details. Mia and Charlie had been close in age and always the best of friends. Worse, Mia's fiancé had died in the same tragic accident with Charlie. Some days, Tess wondered how Mia managed to keep going.

"Hey, girls." Rylee, their youngest sister, hesitated before sitting down. "Eliana, do you want to sit on the end?"

"Sure don't." Eliana grinned. "That will give people ample opportunity to make me get up and go to the kitchen, and I'm supposed to be off duty."

"We could've eaten somewhere else tonight." Rylee settled into the space beside Mia. "We didn't have to meet here."

"It's fine. I was kidding. Kelly's my assistant manager right now and she's doing an outstanding job." Eliana's bright-eyed gaze slid around the table. "I'm so glad you all are here. It makes my heart happy to have my sisters with me."

They spontaneously clasped hands around the table. Another wave of unexpected emotion crested. Tess blinked back more tears, especially when she saw the sheen of moisture in her sisters' eyes. "It makes my heart happy, too," she finally whispered.

Rylee cleared her throat. "I thought business might slow down for you now that Labor Day weekend is over, but things seem like they're pretty steady."

Bless her for changing the subject. The heaviness blanketing their huddle dissipated. Tess reached for one of the laminated menus in the center of the varnished wood table.

"Things haven't really slowed down at all." Eliana handed Mia a menu. "Which is awesome."

"Tell me about it," Rylee said. "We're booked solid until the end of the month. Such a great finale to a wonderful summer."

Rylee was the youngest employee and the only female pilot at Hearts Bay Aviation. She spent her days flying tourists all over the island and beyond. Ever since a popular magazine featured photographs of a local wedding, more and more couples had traveled to Hearts Bay to get married beside the island's giant heart-shaped rock formation.

"I'm so proud of you, El." Tess slung her arm around Eliana's shoulders and pressed her head against her sister's. "I never imagined you'd have your own business at the ripe old age of twenty-five."

"Thank you. Just to clarify, I don't own the building. I wish I did, but you know how that goes. He who shouldn't be named still owns the place and he won't budge."

Laughter rippled around the table at Eliana's stubborn refusal to mention her landlord's name, especially since the guy's son had been her childhood friend. Tess wasn't happy to hear that Eliana was still locked in the same old stalemate, but conversations like this in the restaurant's familiar corner booth made her grateful she'd come home. As Eliana shared a funny story about one of her recent customers, Tess felt the tension knotting her muscles lessen a smidge. That ominous prickle had vanished, too. She must've just been nervous about starting her new job.

"Hey, Tess." Rylee interrupted the conversation and her face paled as she recognized someone through the window outside the restaurant. "Would now be a good time to mention that Asher is here?"

Tess's stomach plummeted as the door opened and Asher Hale walked back into her life.

Chapter Two

He couldn't look away from her if he wanted to.

Asher stood inside the door of the café. His gaze locked with Tess's. Even after seven years, her ability to disarm him with one look hadn't faded. The bell on the door jingled as someone stepped inside, hesitated, then brushed past him. Asher's sneakers remained firmly rooted to the faded linoleum in the entryway. Every customer in the place had swiveled in their seats, their curious stares flitting between him and the booth filled with the Madden sisters in the opposite corner.

Tess tipped her chin up, sending a curtain of her dark silky hair swinging forward. The surprise in her wide-set, golden-brown eyes morphed into irritation. He couldn't blame her. Nothing about this encounter was easy.

He quickly surveyed the restaurant. From the tempting aroma of burgers sizzling on the grill, to the delicious pies and cookies displayed in the bakery case, it was easy to see why the place was packed.

Stealing a quick glance toward the counter, he hoped his order would be waiting for him. Instead, a familiar woman stood beside the register, giving him the death stare over the rim of her dark-framed glasses. Kelly. A woman who used to live across the street from his parents. Evidently he'd somehow offended her. Which was odd, since he hadn't seen her since he'd left Hearts Bay seven years ago.

"May I help you?" she asked, in a tone that implied she'd rather not help. At all.

"Uh, yes. I'm picking up an order for Hale, please."

Her mouth formed a distasteful frown. She sighed, then turned toward the service window separating the dining room from the kitchen. "Order for Hale?" she yelled, loud enough for the entire island to hear.

His face heated. So much for popping in and popping back out. Letting Mom choose the restaurant where one of Tess's sisters had worked for years was a major misstep on his part. At least four other places on the island served fries and burgers. He should've known this wouldn't go well. That game Cameron played on Asher's phone would only hold his attention for so long. If he had to wait much longer, Cameron might weasel out of his car seat before his grandmother could stop him and come inside.

Asher definitely wasn't ready for that.

They'd been here less than a week and he'd avoided running into his son's mother. Just when he'd relaxed, assumed they wouldn't cross paths, he'd spotted her through the open doorway of a classroom during his visit to Cameron's new school today. A half dozen scenarios about how Cameron and Tess's reunion might play out had zinged through his head on repeat all afternoon. They all made Asher feel a thousand times worse for secretly raising their son on his own. Except he didn't regret his decision to intervene and keep Cameron from being placed with an adoptive family. Given the opportunity, he wouldn't change a thing about the last seven years. Tess had made her decision and he'd made his. He'd done what was best for his boy.

Kelly turned back toward him, her frigid gaze sizing him up. "It's going to be a few minutes."

"Great." Asher forced a polite smile. "Thanks."

He palmed the back of his neck and looked at Tess again. He had to say hi. Even with their complicated history, they could handle a brief chat. Right? Thankfully, people had resumed their conversations and stopped staring. He gathered his courage and crossed the dining room toward her booth.

Adrenaline hummed in his veins as she leaned in close and whispered something to her sisters. This was Tess, the girl he'd loved for as long as he could remember, until she broke his heart. They hadn't been Christians. His own relationship with the Lord didn't develop until he was a single dad with a toddler and a friend invited him to church. Still, he'd offered to marry her once they'd found out she was pregnant. Her refusal had crushed his dreams of building a family and a future together. That heartache had driven him to make the most critical decision of his young life.

He shed the ominous thoughts and stopped beside the booth, inches away from Tess. She stared up at him, her spine ramrod straight, but said nothing. Eliana cleared her throat and shot her sisters a look he had zero hope of interpreting.

"Hey." He croaked out the word. Man, that sounded lousy. "How've you been?"

Okay, also lousy.

"Hello, Asher." Not even a hint of a smile. "What are you doing here?"

Huh. He shifted from one foot to the other, then jammed his hands in his pockets. She didn't need to jump up and hug him or anything, but he could do without the disdainful look.

He risked glancing at each of her sisters. Eliana and Mia wore the same frigid you're-not-wanted-here expressions. "Ladies, it's nice to see you all again."

Really? Eliana's arched brow silently questioned the validity of his statement. Mia ignored him and poured herself a glass of water from the carafe in the middle of the table. Only Rylee offered a small polite smile. "Hey, Asher. Congratulations on your new job. That's—"

She flinched, then trailed off and reached under the table. "Ouch, stop kicking me."

He bit back a smile at Tess's not-so-subtle attempt to get Rylee to stop complimenting him. This was even more awkward than he'd expected. He sensed the weight of more disapproving stares boring into his back. A rivulet of fear slid along his spine. Had somebody shared the truth with Tess already? Surely if she'd figured out that Cameron was her son, she'd have more to say to him right now.

"Order for Hale," Kelly called out from somewhere behind him.

"That's me." He offered a weak smile and backed away slowly. "Take care."

"You, too." Something undecipherable flashed across Tess's features. Relief? Hurt? He couldn't be sure, and he wasn't about to ask for clarification.

The disapproval emanating from the corner booth was strong enough to power the entire island. Too bad they couldn't convert some of that negativity into reusable energy. He offered a polite nod to a couple of former classmates eating dinner at a nearby table. In return, they offered the same barely disguised disapproval.

What in the world?

He didn't bother trying to make small talk with Kelly while she plunked three Styrofoam containers on the counter.

"May I have a bag, please?"

She sighed, then tucked the containers inside a plastic sack with Harbor Lights Café's logo printed on the outside.

Asher paid, then put his wallet away and collected the food. "Have a good night."

"You, too."

He turned and strode toward the door without glancing at Tess again.

Outside the café a cold rain spattered his face. A soupy fog had descended, blanketing the hills and mountains that ringed the marina. Asher hurried toward his truck with his shoulders hunched and the takeout nestled against his chest. He opened the door, then climbed inside and passed the bag to his mother.

"So that went well," he grumbled, slamming the door shut.

"Did you get my fries, Daddy?" Cameron asked from the back seat. "And the ketchup?"

"Sure did, buddy. We'll eat as soon as we get back to Grammie's house."

His mother wouldn't look at him. She set the bag at her feet and reached for her seat belt. "Did you run into anyone interesting?"

"Tess and her sisters." Asher clicked his own safety belt in place, then jammed the gear shift into Reverse. He shot her another look as he checked his mirrors before backing out of the parking space. She stared out her window and fidgeted with the strap on her purse.

"It might've been nice to know she was here, Mom."

She squirmed in the passenger seat but still didn't answer him. He should let it go. Provoking her wouldn't change the circumstances. Besides, this was a dangerous topic to discuss with Cameron around. Asher started his new job soon, Cameron was already enrolled in school, and the two of them had settled in at his father's rental property. They couldn't pick up and move back to Oregon, but he wasn't convinced he could handle living this close to Tess without telling her the truth about Cameron.

Over the years, he'd wrestled with the decision not to tell her that he was raising their son. Living in another state had provided the luxury of avoiding the dilemma. But now, with all of them living on the same island, how much longer could he afford to punt?

"Did you know Tess had moved back and that she's a teacher at Cameron's school?" He flicked on the windshield wipers and eased to a stop at the edge of the café's parking lot.

His mother dragged her gaze to meet his. "Cameron's school?"

"What about my school?" Cameron asked, raising his voice to be heard above the frenetic soundtrack of the game on Asher's phone. "Am I still going tomorrow?"

"You're all set for tomorrow, little dude. No worries there." Asher waited for a vehicle to drive by and shot his mother an imploring look. Warning bells clanged in his head. They had to tread carefully here, especially with Cameron listening. He wasn't about to let Mom off the hook, though. She excelled at knowing everything about everyone in Hearts Bay. It was hard to believe she hadn't known that Tess had returned.

"I'd heard she'd interviewed, but I wasn't certain she'd get the job," she said.

"Well, she did. And she's teaching across the hall from Cameron's class."

"Oh, then he must have Mrs. Franklin. She's a wonderful teacher." Mom flipped down the visor and examined her reflection in the tiny lighted mirror.

Asher merged onto Main Street and fought the urge to say something he shouldn't. She was a master of evasiveness.

"Wait. You know my teacher, Grammie?" Cameron giggled. "That's so weird."

"Of course I do, silly." She flashed Cameron a smile. "I know just about everyone."

"And everything that goes on around here," Asher added. "Which is why I can't believe you missed the breaking news."

His mother's smile vanished. "You don't have to be grumpy about it. This is a big island, and there's plenty of room for everybody. If you're so worried, why not transfer him to the other elementary school?"

She couldn't be serious. "School starts tomorrow, Mom. Besides, Dad's house is zoned for Hearts Bay Elementary. I can't request a transfer now."

"I hate to say I told you so, but I tried to warn you that renting from your father wasn't a good idea. If you change your mind, you and Cameron are welcome to move in with me."

Anger burned through his gut. *Don't go there. You'll only regret it.* His parents' contentious divorce was one conversation topic he simply had to avoid. His father's place was great. A nice, fenced yard, three bedrooms and within walking distance to Cameron's school. Now that his dad spent most of his time in Arizona, he was glad to have Asher and Cameron staying in the rental property he owned in Hearts Bay. Mom was probably bitter that she hadn't gotten her way. Asher clicked on his blinker, then turned down the side street toward her house.

"It's not just Tess and her sisters, Mom. It was everybody in the café. They glared at me like I'd kicked their puppy or something."

"Kicked the puppy?" Cameron shrieked. "You can't do that, Daddy."

Oh, brother. This was the longest car ride of his life. "It's an expression. I didn't kick anything."

His mother remained silent. Suspiciously silent.

"Mom, what aren't you telling me?"

She looked out her window again. "There may have been a few…rumors."

"What rumors?"

"You know, the usual gossip that circulates after someone moves away."

Asher stuffed down an impatient groan. "What rumors, Mom? Tell me. Now. Unless…"

Unless they were about Cameron. He rarely asked about his mother. When he did, Asher had always placated him with truthful but vague comments. She'd been nineteen when he was born, and she loved him very much, but she had some things to figure out. Cameron had seemed to accept Asher's explanation.

Those responses wouldn't be enough much longer, not if Tess and Cameron spent hours in the same building five days a week. He couldn't keep the truth concealed forever.

His mom faced him. Her pale features gave him pause.

"Are you all right?" He tapped the brake pedal. "Is it your blood sugar?"

"I told people that you had met someone else right after Tess, eloped and that she had a honeymoon baby." Her voice broke as the words tumbled out. "I was only trying to help."

Icy fingers of dread squeezed his heart. "You're kidding."

"At least I created an alibi." She lowered her voice and leaned across the console. "Which is better than your father's ridiculous plan. He thought shipping you off to your sister's house was so brilliant. I told him someday you'd have to face these people again, but he wouldn't listen. You should thank me."

Oh, this was getting more convoluted by the minute. No wonder Tess and her sisters, the whole café, really, had given him such disgusted looks. "I'm almost afraid to ask, but I've got to know. Where is this fictional someone now?"

"That's the best part." She clutched his arm. There was that mischievous gleam in her eyes again. "She left you for another guy. Isn't that great? Now you're the heroic single dad."

"No, Mom. I'm not." Asher white-knuckled the steering wheel and spots peppered his vision. "The whole town probably thinks I'm a cheater."

* * *

"Sixteen students are reading below grade level?" Tess scanned the email on her laptop. "That's more than I expected."

"Those are only the kids we've identified so far." Courtney, the second-grade teaching assistant, hoisted herself onto the counter behind Tess's desk. "We have assessed none of the fourth-, fifth- and sixth-graders yet."

"So there might be more." Tess grabbed a pen and flipped open her planner. "If I work with some in a small group, bring two in at a time while my students are at art, PE and music, then schedule the rest after school, I might be able to squeeze everyone into a weekly rotation."

"Sounds intense." Courtney picked at chipped polish on her fingernail. "Once you review their assessments and let me know what you need, I'm happy to help."

Tess nodded, scrolling down the list. Her breath hitched when she read Cameron Hale's name. *Oh no.* Not Asher's son. After their painful and awkward interaction at the café last week, she'd tried hard not to think about him. Her sisters had coached her to play it cool once he'd stepped inside, but as soon as he started walking toward their booth, all the old hurt came rushing back. The force of her anger had surprised her. Stolen her words. She hadn't meant to be rude, but she refused to pretend she was happy to see him. Especially since Cameron's appearance confirmed the stories she'd heard. Asher Hale, the boy she'd loved since she'd been a student at this same school, had been unfaithful.

"Has anyone mentioned last year's abysmal test scores?" Courtney's leather boots thumped against the cabinets. "Second-grade test scores were the worst they've been in five years."

Tess clicked the end of her pen. "That's rough."

"There are a couple in Mrs. Franklin's class that are struggling with basic sight words."

"Is Cameron Hale one of those?"

She hadn't meant to be so direct. Really, she hadn't.

Courtney's mouth twitched. "I wondered when you were going to ask."

Tess feigned annoyance. "I need to know."

"Sure you do." Courtney winked. "What else would you like to know? His dad's marital status? Where they're living?"

Tess crumpled a piece of scratch paper into a ball and chucked it at her.

Courtney batted it away, laughing. "All right, all right. Cameron struggles with fluency and comprehension. He'd benefit from one-on-one attention."

Super. That's what she was afraid of. "Has anyone notified the parents yet?"

"Letters will go home in their communication folders. I can't speak for the other teachers, but Mrs. Franklin has already invited parents in for conferences."

"Oh, good." Tess made a note in her planner. "I'll ask her if she wants me to sit in on those."

"If you want to speak with Cameron's dad, he'll be here at lunch."

Tess's pen slid from her fingers and clattered onto the linoleum at her feet.

"Cameron's a cute kid," Courtney said. "Asher's still quite handsome as well."

"I hadn't noticed."

"Ha." Courtney smoothed her hand down her long auburn ponytail. "Nice try."

Heat climbed her neck. Courtney had been two years behind her in Eliana's class all through school and had a propensity to say exactly what she thought. On more than one occasion, Eliana and Courtney had exchanged heated words. Tess didn't want to react, but she'd never been good at hiding her emotions, either.

"That was a long time ago."

"Nothing wrong with a little second-chance romance."

Tess retrieved her pen. "The kids will be finished with music soon. I need to use the restroom before I pick them up."

"I'll get your students and bring them back here." Courtney hopped off the counter. "It's no problem."

"Okay." Tess offered a smile. Maybe she'd been a bit harsh. "Thank you."

"Anytime."

After Courtney left, Tess reviewed the list of students who needed help. Her gaze landed on Cameron's name again. She wasn't proud of her behavior when Asher spoke to her at the café last week. Even though in the moment it felt like the entire town was watching their not-so-happy reunion, and her sisters, too, that didn't excuse her lousy attitude.

She'd have to do better.

She stared out the window at the gray-blue ocean in the distance, kicking up spray as the waves smacked the rocky shoreline.

Courtney's comments had bothered her. Not just the part about Asher, but her observation that working with sixteen students a week in addition to her regular classroom teaching sounded intense.

Perhaps that was too lofty a goal.

She couldn't stand the thought of these kids slipping through the cracks. Literacy was a crucial skill and she'd do everything in her power to make sure all the students placed in her care were reading at or above grade level. The school needed her skills and expertise. Her education and additional certification as a reading specialist meant she was more than capable to do the job they'd hired her to do.

Frankly, the extra income in her paycheck for being a reading specialist wouldn't hurt. Living in Hearts Bay cost more than she remembered, probably because she hadn't worried about groceries, rent and gas prices when she relied on her parents for everything. She had agreed to split the rent and utilities at the house she shared with Eliana, but her monthly expenses were still going to be higher than she'd expected.

She weaved through the pods of desks and hurried down the hall to the staff restroom. The aroma of lunch preparation in the cafeteria wafted toward her.

If you want to speak with Cameron's dad, he'll be here at lunch.

More crucial information courtesy of Courtney. This single detail made Tess more nervous than the first time Asher had asked her to dance back in high school. She'd have to get used to the idea of seeing him and Cameron regularly. No matter what Asher had said or done in the past, she'd treat him and Cameron the same as everyone else—with kindness and respect. Uncertainty gnawed at her as she glimpsed her reflection in the bathroom mirror. A crevice marred her brow. Was accepting this job another decision she'd regret?

Six days in and he'd already been summoned to Cameron's school. This couldn't be good. Asher's stomach tightened as he stepped inside Mrs. Franklin's classroom.

"Thanks for coming by today, Asher." Mrs. Franklin smiled, then rounded her desk and sat down. "Please have a seat."

Asher claimed the metal folding chair she'd positioned in front of her desk and dragged his sweaty palms across his khaki cargo pants. He'd stopped by on his lunch break from work to meet with her because she'd asked him to. Something about checking in and making sure Cameron's year was off to a good start. Her kind words and soothing tone on the phone hadn't made him any less concerned.

She clasped her hands on top of an orange folder in the center of her well-organized desk and met his gaze. "How are things going with Cameron? Are you getting settled in your new place?"

"Everything seems fine so far. Moving requires a ton of time and attention to detail. It's kind of overwhelming, to be honest. I've tried to be patient with Cameron, but I haven't been able to give him my full attention. This is the first time we've lived alone, just the two of us, so we're still trying to find our groove."

Man, why did he feel the need to tell her his entire life story?

"So you used to live with someone else?"

"My sister, Krista. You probably remember her. She's a pediatrician and her husband's an anesthesiologist. We lived with them in Oregon for almost seven years. It helped to have extra sets of hands around, you know?" He sat up straighter in his chair, wishing he could snatch that last sentence back. "Not that I can't handle being a single dad, but sometimes it's easier knowing there's somebody there for backup."

Mrs. Franklin nodded. "I completely understand. My daughter has two children now and her youngest is a newborn. My husband and I spend quite a bit of time helping. Having family close by is so important."

His mother and her stricken expression when she'd confessed to the rumors she had spread about him flitted through his mind. An image of Tess chased those thoughts. He didn't want to think about either one of them. He still couldn't believe his mother had done such a thing. Although, as much as he hated to admit it, she was right about one thing. His father's scheme for sending Asher to Oregon with a newborn baby had been ridiculous. Especially the fake adoption papers their family's attorney somehow convinced Tess to sign. Moving back to Hearts Bay meant facing the same people who'd known him his whole life. They were bound to have questions. Maybe he'd been so blinded by the opportunity to land the job of his dreams that he hadn't given enough thought to what people might say when he showed up with a seven-year-old.

C'mon. Focus.

Cameron and the reason for this meeting was all that mattered right now. Asher had already promised himself on the drive over that he'd do whatever Mrs. Franklin asked. Well, almost anything. Okay, so he wouldn't be the first parent in line to volunteer inside the classroom, but he'd happily sign up to chaperone a field trip or two.

"I've been able to spend a little time with Cameron one-on-one, and Courtney, the second-grade teaching assistant, has spent some time with him as well."

Asher played with the zipper on his vest. He didn't like that her expression had turned serious.

"I invited you in to hear more about how things are going at home, and to share some observations."

"Observations?" Asher grew still. "What do you mean?"

Mrs. Franklin glanced down at the folder and flipped it open. "How do you think Cameron's doing with his independent reading? If you read together at home, what kind of books does he like? When you take him to the library, what kind of books does he want to check out?"

The library. Asher let his gaze drift toward the window. The library was probably the last place Asher would take an active boy like Cameron. He'd have to tell him not to climb the shelves or jump on the furniture. Not to mention getting him to whisper was next to impossible.

"Asher?" Mrs. Franklin prompted. "Do you read to Cameron at home?"

"Sometimes." When he wasn't too exhausted.

"Have you ever noticed him mixing up similar letters like *B*s and *D*s or writing his numbers backward?"

Wait. What? A headache formed behind Asher's eyes. He tried to recall any of Cameron's schoolwork that he'd saved from first grade. "A few times with his math worksheets."

An especially tough night resurfaced in Asher's mind. Cameron had flung his pencil across the room, then raced down the hall to his bedroom, wailing about his math worksheet. Asher's brother-in-law had been there and had helped him reassure Cameron that he'd be able to figure out his math problems. The crisis had passed, and they'd all moved on, but Asher hadn't forgotten his sweet boy's frustration. "We've had some issues," he finally admitted.

"Any family history of learning disabilities?"

Her question landed like a punch in the gut. "Not that I know of."

Mrs. Franklin nodded, then slid the paper in front of her aside.

"Mrs. Franklin, I don't mean to be rude, but you're worrying me. You've known our family for years. If there's something wrong..."

He trailed off, fighting to keep the emotion from creeping into his voice. *Just say it. Whatever it is, please tell me.*

"Asher, it's because I know you and your family that I called you." Mrs. Franklin leaned forward and smiled gently, but the empathy reflected in her features did little to ease Asher's anxiety. "It's my job to keep you informed. I've identified some behavior with Cameron that's common among kids who aren't reading fluently."

"Are you implying that Cameron's dyslexic?"

She hesitated. "That's not for me to diagnose."

"So you're saying he might be?" An icy chill skated across Asher's spine. How did he miss this?

"I'm saying Cameron likely needs further evaluation, possibly by an expert outside the school district."

"I—I don't understand. We read to him. Not as much as we should have, but we tried. I thought boys developed slower than girls. Isn't it normal for most second-grade boys to be behind?"

"Cameron is a delightful little boy, Asher. He's helpful and eager to please. He also seems to know a lot about animals and insects, especially dinosaurs."

"He's really into dinosaurs."

"I noticed." Mrs. Franklin chuckled. "He's shared a fun fact every single day."

Asher pushed his fingers through his hair. "Obviously he can retain information. We're not concerned about that. Are we?" His voice hitched up. He barely sounded like himself and his insides churned like the wake behind a fishing boat.

"No one is questioning your parenting." She handed him an official-looking piece of paper from Cameron's previous elementary school. "This is hard news to handle. Here's some information that came with Cameron from his first-grade teacher."

Asher accepted the letter printed on paper with a familiar letterhead. *Oh no.* Cameron's first-grade teacher had offered an end-of-year parent-teacher conference, but he'd been overwhelmed at work, juggling a big presentation along with traveling to a training session in Washington, DC. He'd declined the meeting, then forgotten to reschedule. Since they'd moved, he hadn't given that missed meeting a second thought. Until now.

The paper trembled in his hand as he quickly scanned it. He winced when he read the final sentence recommending further assessments and intervention. This made little sense. They'd lived with Krista since Cameron was a newborn. She'd never mentioned concerns about his development.

Had she?

Asher returned the letter to Mrs. Franklin, then scrubbed his fingers along his jaw. "What's your recommendation? Should I hire a tutor?"

She tucked the letter inside the folder and closed it. "The most important thing is to intervene and intervene early. That's fancy language for identifying the problem and taking steps to get some help. Your job is to make reading fun and set a good example."

"Fun?"

"Yes, fun. If reading is a chore or a hassle, then Cameron will resist. Make a game of picking out words he can identify on the back of the cereal box, draw letters with shaving cream on a cookie sheet, sing funny rhyming songs, listen to audiobooks and read, read, read together."

Oh, boy. Cameron sagged back in his chair. Shaving cream? Games? This sounded overwhelming. And messy. Since they'd moved back to Hearts Bay, he'd been swimming in a sea of incomplete tasks. Of course he wanted to help Cameron get back on track, but these days it was all he could do to work, get Cameron to and from school on time, then tackle the essential chores before falling into bed every night exhausted.

"I can see I've given you a lot to ponder." Mrs. Franklin pushed back her chair and stood. "The good news is, we're here to help. Ms. Madden was hired as a second-grade teacher and she's certified as a reading specialist. I recommend she work with Cameron twice a week until you can make an appointment for further evaluation."

Asher squeezed his eyes shut, overcome by Mrs. Franklin's so-called good news. *Tess.* Twice a week. Please, no.

"Further evaluation?" He opened his eyes and pushed out the words. "Where?"

"You'll need to schedule an appointment with your

new pediatrician. In my experience, he or she completes a vision screening, a hearing test, and often gives a recommendation for psychological testing. That will require a trip off island, I'm afraid, but don't worry. We'll connect you with a reputable provider in Kenai or Anchorage."

Mrs. Franklin hovered in the doorway. She turned back and motioned for him to follow. "Come with me. We'll pop across the hall and speak to Ms. Madden before the kids come inside from recess."

Asher stood and trudged after her, his head spinning with all the reasons why Tess was not the solution for Cameron's issues. Sure, she was a teacher and more than qualified to help Cameron learn to read. But she was also his mother and didn't know it. If he agreed to this arrangement, he'd eventually have to tell her. Cameron, too. The thought nearly brought him to his knees. All his well-ordered plans and good intentions to look out for his mother and make a life for his son in this town he'd loved so much would mean nothing when Tess found out the truth.

Chapter Three

"Miss Madden?" Mrs. Franklin hovered in the classroom doorway. Asher stood behind her, his expression pinched. "Do you have a minute?"

Tess's fork slid from her fingers and clattered into the disposable salad container, splashing Italian dressing onto the mustard yellow sweater she'd begged Eliana to let her borrow. Tess sighed and stood quickly. "Yeah, hi. I mean, come in. I was..." She tried for a smile. "Making a mess of my lunch. Give me one second."

Asher was here. Now. Her pulse skittered and flailed like a kid learning to ice-skate. Clearly her heart never received the memo that the man was no longer an option.

She grabbed a paper towel from the dispenser on the wall, added water from the sink, then gently dabbed at the stains on the fabric. Eliana was going to clobber her if she'd ruined a brand-new sweater.

"We're sorry to interrupt." Mrs. Franklin moved toward her. Asher hung back, his blue eyes roaming the classroom. Tess noted the stubborn lock of coffee-brown hair swooping across his forehead, just as it always had. His forest green long-sleeved shirt and navy blue down vest emphasized his athletic frame in a way that caught her attention. Courtney's observations about him were spot on. He'd matured. The boy she'd been infatuated with had matured into a man. A handsome man who filled the doorway and sent her brain careening around dangerous curves, offering memories she had zero business recalling. Especially if he belonged to someone else.

"Asher Hale stopped by for a quick chat about his son, Cameron." Mrs. Franklin offered her trademark smile. Was that a gleam in her eye? Tess couldn't be certain. Surely this wasn't some sort of bizarre matchmaking attempt. If so, Tess would have to remind her that ship had sailed.

Besides, no one had confirmed whether Asher and his wife were divorced. Eliana had mentioned that's what Asher's mother had told everyone, but Tess was still curious. Her eyes slid to his left hand, which he'd conveniently tucked out of sight in the pocket of his khaki pants.

"Tess?" Mrs. Franklin's voice pulled her back to the present. She met Asher's gaze. He'd caught her staring. Except he looked less than amused. Two pink splotches of color hugged his cheekbones. If she wasn't mistaken, he looked worried.

She tossed the paper towel in the trash can beside her desk, then clasped her hands in front of her. "What can I do for you?"

"Asher's son, Cameron, is one of my students who needs extra support with reading comprehension."

"Yes, of course. Happy to help."

Behind Mrs. Franklin, Asher's brows lifted. Was he

doubting her? Her stomach tightened. How rude. What had happened to the sweet fun-loving boy she'd fallen in love with all those years ago when they'd roamed the halls of this same building?

Mrs. Franklin's gaze pinged between them. "Cameron will be in Tess's very capable hands."

Tess acknowledged the compliment with a gracious smile. "Do you have any information from his last school?"

"Oh, I left his file on my desk." Mrs. Franklin checked her watch. "Look at the time. I'd better help Courtney bring the kids in from recess and let you two work out the details."

"Wait," Tess called after her. "We need to talk about his assessment and proper intervention strategies."

"We talked about that. Asher can update you." She patted his arm as she brushed past him. "I've got to run."

"Sure you do," Tess mumbled, staring after her retreating form.

Asher cleared his throat and shifted from one foot to the other. Her classroom seemed uncomfortably hot. She blew out a long breath. How sad that neither of them knew what to say to each other. She used to tell him everything.

Outside, a muffled whistle blew, signaling the end of recess. Tess peeked through the large windows beside her desk. Courtney stood in the middle of the playground, wearing a red satchel over one shoulder for any minor emergencies. She and another teaching assistant herded the students toward the door. Thankfully, Tess wouldn't have to endure making conversation with Asher for long because her kids would come inside soon. "Recess is over. I need to get ready for my next lesson. Do you have questions, Asher?"

"Too many to count. This is…" He ran his fingertips across his forehead, then leaned against the doorframe. "This is a lot to process."

Was she supposed to feel sorry for him?

"When would you like to start Cameron's sessions?" She reached for her planner. "I don't have any other students scheduled yet, so you can choose which afternoons work best."

"I left my phone in my truck. I'll have to get back to you."

The defeated tone wasn't one she'd often heard from the happy, optimistic version of Asher she'd once known. And loved. She studied him. "Are you all right?"

"Mrs. Franklin basically told me Cameron can't read. So no, I'm not okay."

Tess stopped short of asking if he'd rather speak to his wife first. In her experience, sometimes fathers wanted the mothers to take the lead on scheduling appointments and intervention strategies. Selfishly, she didn't really want to know anything about that relationship, though. The less she communicated with the woman who stole her boyfriend, the better.

Embarrassed by the immature battle waging in her head, she turned back toward her desk and tore a piece of paper from her personalized notepad. The muffled sound of footsteps tromping across the asphalt outside the school prompted her to act quickly. She grabbed a pen and scrawled her email address across the top along with Tuesday and Thursday afternoons from three thirty to four thirty.

"Here." She crossed the room and handed Asher the paper. "I'm available for an hour after school on Tuesdays and Thursdays. Think about it and let me know."

"Thanks." He took the note and folded it in half. "Are you sure you're going to be okay with this?"

"Okay with what?"

"Working with Cameron."

"Why wouldn't I be?"

A muscle in his jaw ticked. "It's a fair question, Tess."

"Fair?" She fisted her hands on her hips. "You're implying that I can't be professional because you and I dated eons ago. I'd hardly call that fair."

Asher's olive skin blanched white. "Dated, huh?"

"Yes, *dated*."

His Adam's apple bobbed as he swallowed hard. "That's an interesting synopsis of our relationship."

Tension arced between them, forcing her to step back. She bumped into a student's desk, lost her balance and had to claw at the edge of the desk to keep from falling. Her face flamed. She hated that he'd flustered her with his stupid loaded questions. Half-tempted to lob a snarky comment, she opted to take the high road and remain silent. He'd betrayed *her*. Everyone knew that. She would not waste her time getting tangled in a petty argument.

She raised her chin. "The kids are coming in. You'd better go before Cameron sees you."

He straightened and turned to leave, then faced her again. "There's one more thing. Tess, you—"

"Asher, please. Just go." Her fingers itched to push him out the door. She couldn't handle the sound of him saying her name. Not for one more second. And if Cameron saw his father in the hallway, the little guy would probably have a dozen questions and a tough time focusing for the rest of the day. "Send me a message when you're ready to get started. Cameron will need to come to my classroom right after school and you'll need to arrange for him to be picked up. I can commit to six weeks, which should give you plenty of time to find a pediatrician and schedule an appointment with a specialist."

"Got it," Asher said, his expression grim. He held up the note. "Thanks again. I'll be in touch."

He left, barely slipping out of sight before the kids filed into the hallway from recess. Tess darted around the room, putting her unfinished lunch away, then working quickly to set out the bins of brightly colored manipulatives for the afternoon math lesson. The entire time, memories of Asher played in her head. A highlight reel of their childhood crush blossoming into what she'd once believed would be a forever kind of love. Especially after they'd survived a grueling separation while he was away at college in Oregon. He was two years older and determined to be a wildlife biologist. She'd been equally determined to wait for him. He could be whatever he wanted, as long as they were together.

Then everything changed the night she got pregnant. Asher had been home for the summer break from college and they'd let their emotions drive them into uncharted territory. As the months passed, Tess grew more certain adoption would give all involved the future they deserved, but Asher refused to agree with her. In her weaker moments, she regretted that the child they'd created had ultimately driven them apart.

Her students' exuberant chatter grew louder. She

banished all thoughts of Asher and forced a smile as she welcomed the kids back into the classroom. The hurt and regret from the past didn't have to control her. Since her college roommate had taught her what it meant to know and follow Jesus, she'd grown to understand that her faith set her free from the things that had once held her captive. Being back in Hearts Bay didn't mean she had to surrender to the same old pain.

"I. Want. Grammie." Cameron flung himself face-down on the black leather couch, sobs racking his body.

Oh, boy. Asher stood in the middle of the living room, hands on his hips, mentally scrounging for any hot tips to navigate Cameron's latest epic meltdown. Mrs. Franklin's words of wisdom flitted through his head. So far, her advice hadn't worked. Reading together was the opposite of fun.

"Grammie will read to me. I know she will." The cushions muffled Cameron's words, but the message was crystal clear. His son didn't want to read with him. Or do much of anything together. They'd butted heads like two bull moose ever since Asher had picked him up from the local rec center's after-school program. Mom's chocolate chip cookies must've erased Cameron's hurt feelings from her thoughtless comments. Or maybe he was just that desperate to hang out with someone other than mean old Dad. Ouch.

"Here's the thing, pal." He fought to keep his voice even. Calm and reassuring. "You're supposed to be reading while I listen."

Cameron sprung from the couch like it was on fire, then swept the books stacked on the coffee table onto the floor. "These ones are stupid."

"Cameron James Hale, books are not stupid. Pick those up, please."

"No." Cameron swiped at the tears on his splotchy cheeks. "You can't make me."

Lord, give me patience. This kid is jumping on my last nerve. "If you can't obey, then you're going straight to bed after dinner. No more screen time."

Which punished them both, because he'd been looking forward to their latest ritual of watching their new favorite baking show together.

Cameron's eyes welled with fresh tears. "I have to see Grammie, though."

His pathetic expression made Asher's heart hurt. The poor fella was having a tough time. Still, he couldn't back down from consistent boundaries. And a visit from his mother wasn't the solution to his parenting dilemmas.

"Grammie isn't coming over tonight."

"Yes, she is." Cameron ran to the window and pressed his palm to the glass. The house they were renting from his father had wide windows in the living room facing a flat yard on a quiet street. A much better arrangement than the tiny postage-stamp lawn outside the town house they'd shared with Krista and her husband in Oregon.

"She said it was our special secret. A Wednesday surprise."

Asher stifled a groan. Secrets and surprises. Two of his mother's favorite things.

"Cam—"

"There she is. Daddy, look. I see her car." Cameron grinned. "I knew she'd come."

"Are you sure that's not the neighbor's car?"

The older couple living across the street drove a vehicle the same color as his mother's.

"She's pulling in the driveway." Cameron swiped his sleeve across his cheeks, then darted around him. "I'll let her in."

Asher trailed after him out the front door and onto the cement steps.

"Hi, boys." Sharon emerged from her silver SUV. She'd styled her short dark hair in funky spikes, and animal-print feather-shaped earrings dangled from her ears as she rounded the front of her vehicle. Her black heels clicked on the asphalt and the hem of her long black tunic rippled against her black leather pants. Why did she dress up when she typically ran her travel agent business from her spare bedroom? He wouldn't say a word, though. He'd choose his battles wisely.

"I like your outfit, Grammie." Cameron flitted around her like a bee around a blooming flower. "Are those real feathers?"

Mom chuckled and flashed Asher an amused glance. "Nope, not real. But I brought you something *real* yummy."

"What is it?" Cameron giggled, tugging on her sleeve. "Tell us what you brought."

"Hi, Mom." Asher joined her on the passenger side and held the door open while she reached inside. "I didn't know you were coming over."

She handed him a plastic container with a lid, then scooped a reusable grocery bag from the floorboards. "I thought you boys might enjoy my famous tacos."

Asher's stomach growled in agreement.

"Yay!" Cameron cheered and bounded up the steps. Asher offered a weak smile. He was grateful. Really, he was. And a bit relieved. After the afternoon he'd had with Cameron, dinner was the last thing on his mind. Her arrival was a blessing. Even if her good mood and generosity made him nervous.

Inside, the aroma of seasoned chicken filled the cozy kitchen as he popped the lid off the container. Mom quickly unpacked the rest of the meal.

Cameron eyed the package of chips. "Can I have chips and dip?"

"Please wash your hands in the bathroom first," Asher said.

"Okay, Dad." He trotted down the hall, his sneakers slapping on the laminate flooring.

"Wow, he must really like chips." Mom unscrewed the lid on the salsa jar. "Does he need one taco or two?"

"Let's start with one." Asher crossed to the refrigerator to get the milk, then poured a plastic cup full for Cameron.

"Honestly, did your father not leave you a single decent serving spoon?" His mother heaved a disgusted sigh and pawed through the utensils in the drawer.

Asher set the table and refused to comment. He didn't have the energy to engage in that sensitive topic tonight. Or any night. Mom wasn't shy about expressing her bitterness over the divorce. Dad's decision to move to Arizona with his girlfriend didn't help the situation, either. Asher still clung to the desperate hope that he could remain neutral.

"I'm back." Cameron returned, his sweatshirt sleeves pushed up to his elbows. He scrambled onto one of the chairs at the oval table beside the window. "May I please have chips and dip?"

"Yes, you may." Asher carried chips, salsa and

Cameron's cup of milk to the table. "Thank you for using your good manners."

"Yep." Cameron slurped his milk loudly and Asher ruffled his hair. They might have hit a rough patch lately, but he could never stay angry with Cameron for long. He helped plate the rest of the food, then poured two glasses of water and carried them to the table. After he said grace, they dug into the meal.

"So, Cameron." His mom added a dollop of sour cream to her taco salad. "How's school going?"

"Good." The corn shell crunched as he took a giant bite of his taco. Thankfully, Cameron hadn't whined about the food. Tacos usually weren't his favorite. Maybe he was too hungry to complain. Asher rolled his shoulders, trying to release the tension that had camped there all day.

"What's your favorite part?"

"Recess," Cameron mumbled around a mouthful of food.

Mom chuckled. "That was always your dad's favorite, too."

Asher savored the blend of spicy, crunchy flavors and tried not to second-guess his mother's motives. They'd had a frank discussion while Cameron was in school last week about kindness and respect. She'd promised to adjust her attitude and speak kindly. Although he'd heard nothing close to an apology. Was tonight's visit supposed to neutralize some of her missteps?

"Do you like being in Mrs. Franklin's class?" Mom asked.

"It's okay." Cameron's brow furrowed and he looked down at his plate.

Asher stopped chewing. He and his mother exchanged worried glances.

"Just okay?" Mom prodded. "What would make it better?"

"I wish I was in Miss Test's class," Cameron said.

Asher's heart hammered.

"Who?" Mom smiled and reached for her water.

"Miss Madden," Asher said.

Her eyes rounded. "Oh."

"She's prettier." Cameron dragged another chip through his puddle of salsa. "Nicer, too."

Oh no. Asher dropped what was left of his taco on his plate and reached for his water. He chugged the whole glass, his mind racing. Cameron had hardly spent any time with Tess and already he was smitten?

"I'm sure you're going to have a great year," his mother said. "Your school is the best on the island."

Asher pushed his food around on his plate. She had a point, although he couldn't shake the nagging thought that maybe he should've enrolled Cameron elsewhere. Tolerating the inconvenience of driving a little farther to get him to and from school might be worth it if it meant keeping Cameron from crossing paths with Tess. That would require moving to a different house, though. Not happening.

He pushed out a sigh, earning a pointed glance from his mother.

"Grammie, will you read to me before you go?"

"Sure." She scooped another bite of salad onto her fork. "I'd love to read to you."

"I'll get some books." Cameron slid from his chair and raced out of the room. "Let's read the one about dinosaurs and tacos."

Asher didn't bother to call him back to finish eating. He needed a minute with Cameron out of earshot.

"What am I going to do?" He shoved his plate aside. "He adores her already."

"Don't worry." His mother's smile didn't quite reach her eyes. "What's meant to be will be."

"That's what I am worried about," he grumbled. Why trust the advice from someone who'd been complicit in this disaster? He'd tried to do the right thing and intervene to keep Cameron from being placed with an adoptive family. But going along with his father's scheme to trick Tess was wrong. Their actions had kicked up a hefty pile of unintended consequences. He and the people he loved most were caught in an avalanche of dysfunction and lies. How was he supposed to tunnel his way out?

This was a terrible idea. Who said yes to tutoring their ex-boyfriend's kid, anyway? Tess stole a glance at the clock on her classroom wall. Four forty-five. Asher was fifteen minutes late to pick up Cameron. She'd give him five more minutes and then she'd call.

"Do you have anything to eat?" Cameron slumped in his blue plastic chair. "I'm hungry."

"Me, too." Tess stood and crossed the room to her desk. She kept a handful of packaged snacks in her bottom desk drawer for emergencies like this. "Do you have any food allergies?"

"What's a food allergy?" Cameron propped his elbow on the table and leaned his head against his palm. His dark brown hair stuck up in the back like a rooster tail. Her fingers itched to smooth it down. Weird.

"When a person is allergic to something, their body

has a reaction. It's kind of like their body says no thank you and tries to keep the thing out. Do you know anyone who can't eat peanuts or drink milk?" Tess frowned, then selected two packs of graham crackers. She wasn't explaining this very well. Probably because she was hungry and cranky. Asher had a lot of nerve, not showing up on time.

"A kid at my old school didn't eat peanut butter."

"That's probably because he or she was allergic to peanuts." She returned to her seat beside Cameron, then checked the tag on his backpack slouched at his feet. Kids who had allergies kept a special sticker on the ID tag clipped to their backpacks. He was stickerless. Good. So far she'd avoided looking in his file. Not that temptation didn't lurk every time she logged on to her computer. Plenty of questions circulated in her head about Cameron, his mother and the life he'd left behind in Oregon. She wasn't supposed to care about the woman who'd captured Asher's heart and given him a child, but if no one showed to pick him up soon, she'd have to look for his emergency contact information. And once she found those details, it would be difficult to avoid reading the rest of his file.

"Hope you like graham crackers." She set the snack in front of him. "Can you open it?"

He nodded, then ripped the package open. "Do you have any juice boxes?"

"Sorry, no." Tess chuckled. "Plenty of water, though. Would you like some?"

"Water tastes boring." He sighed, then leaned over and grabbed his water bottle from where it had rolled under his chair. "Do you know where my dad is?"

Good question. "I'm sure he'll be here any minute. Tell me some words that start with the letter *g*."

"Gasosaurus, gigantoraptor, gigantosaurus, gemini-raptor..." He paused and took a bite of his cracker.

Tess couldn't help but smile. This kid sure knew his dinosaurs.

Someone knocked on the window and she flinched.

"Daddy!" Cameron giggled and pointed toward the window. "That's a funny face."

Tess swiveled in her chair and followed Cameron's finger. Asher stood outside her classroom, his face pressed to the glass and framed with his cupped hands. He looked less than amused.

"Let's go let him in." Tess stood and gestured for Cameron to come with her. They weaved through the desks, left the classroom and hurried down the hall. What was he doing peering inside her window like a creeper? Why didn't he come into the school like a normal parent?

Asher hovered outside the double doors at the end of the hall. Cameron ran ahead, the metal bar clanging as he slammed into it and shoved the door open.

"Dad, you're here. Finally!" Cameron leaped against Asher, throwing his arms around his waist.

Asher's arms snaked around Cameron's body and pulled him close. "Sorry, pal."

Tess joined them, wrapping her cardigan sweater tighter as an icy wind swirled around her. "You're late."

"I was here on time." Anger flashed in his eyes. "All the doors are locked. I called the front office and it went to voice mail. How am I supposed to pick up my son if I can't get in the building?"

Oh. Tess opened her mouth, then clamped it shut.

She hadn't thought to check if they'd locked him out. She'd assumed the front-office staff stayed until five o'clock, especially when students were still in the building. "I'm sorry, I didn't realize the office was closed already. We'd better exchange phone numbers."

The solution was out of her mouth before she could give it a second thought. Or take it back. Asher acknowledged it with a brief nod, then looked away.

"Let's get my stuff." Cameron tugged on Asher's hand. "Besides, I didn't finish my snack."

"Lead the way." Cameron zipped back inside the building. Tess pressed her back against the door and held it open. She sucked in her breath, acutely aware of Asher's proximity as he passed by without looking at her. An appealing scent of pine and fresh air trailed in his wake, which she was forced to endure all the way back to her classroom. She couldn't ignore the way his dark hair brushed against the collar of his black jacket, or the adorable way he looked down at Cameron while the boy chattered about his day.

Tess's heart squeezed. He was such an attentive father. That thought materialized without her permission. She tucked it out of sight, like an old sweater that didn't fit well but she couldn't bring herself to part with. Hopes and dreams about a future with Asher still waltzed through her head from time to time, as though some small part of her couldn't quite get over him. Couldn't quite move past the memory that they'd created a child together and she'd dashed his hopes of building a family—and a future—with her when she'd refused to marry him.

Stop.

Cameron hustled into her classroom, still sharing

all the details of his day with Asher. "You should have seen me kick the ball in PE, Dad. It went all the way to the back wall and bounced off."

"Yeah?" Asher tucked his hands in his jacket pockets and rocked back on his heels. "Did you run fast?"

"Uh-huh." Cameron jammed his water bottle back in his backpack, then snagged his second graham cracker off the table. "I ran all the way to second base, too. My team won, three to two."

"Way to go." Asher's smile made Tess's knees all wobbly, so she quickly averted her gaze and took the long way to her desk. "How did the reading go today?"

She halted her steps. As much as she wanted him to leave her classroom, she owed him an update on Cameron's session, and her phone number. Drawing a deep breath, she faced him wearing her most professional smile. "He did great."

"Define *great*."

"Oh. Well." She clutched the edges of her cardigan like the seasoned fishermen often clutched their suspenders before they shared their best stories over a cup of coffee at Eliana's café. "He sure knows his dinosaurs. I think I learned a few additional facts today."

Her laughter came out forced and Asher's forehead crinkled. Obviously he wanted a more professional assessment.

"We reviewed sight words and focused on letter-sound relationships. As I'm sure you know, reading requires both decoding and comprehension."

"Right." Asher nodded. "Anything in particular we should work on at home?"

"Keep reading." Tess offered Cameron a thumbs-up. "You've got this, bud."

Cameron shrugged, then moved toward the door. "C'mon, Dad. I want to go home."

Okay, then. Maybe today hadn't gone as well as she'd thought. This was only their first session. Cameron had been compliant and seemed interested in whatever she'd asked him to do so far. He wasn't reading at grade level, but that was understandable at this point.

Asher lingered beside the desk near the doorway, those infernal blue eyes laser focused and making her palms sweat.

"I'll see you next time, then." She shifted from one foot to the other. "Have a good night."

"Your phone number?" He pulled his phone from his pocket. "I'd prefer not to pound on your window again."

"Right. Of course." Tess rattled off the numbers and his fingers flew over the screen, while her brain sailed back in time to all the summer nights when he had tapped on her window to get her to sneak out.

"Thanks." He put his phone away and offered another terse head bob. "See you."

Once they'd left, Tess quickly removed the graham cracker crumbs from the table with an antibacterial wipe. If only she could wipe away her complicated feelings toward Asher. Seeing him brought her past rushing back, forcing her to revisit the hurt and regret she'd worked so hard to banish.

Chapter Four

After the closing prayer, Asher stood and slid out of the pew in the last row at Orca Island Community Church. The worship team remained onstage and played through their final song again, filling the sanctuary with lyrics and music. Familiar faces dotted the pews nearby and he felt the weight of curious glances as he moved toward the exit. He couldn't wait to pick Cameron up from his kids' class, then grab some lunch. Cameron wanted pizza and Asher was more than happy to comply with his request. The sermon was great and all, but hanging around and inviting more icy stares and frigid, stilted conversation wasn't his idea of fellowship.

He smiled politely at the ushers flanking the double doors as he passed, then hurried toward the long hallway on the other side of the atrium that led to the classrooms and nursery.

"Oh, hello, dear." Mrs. Lovell, the mayor's wife and resident wolf in sheep's clothing, stepped into his path. Asher groaned inwardly and slowed his steps to keep from colliding with her. His supervisor at the fish and wildlife commission had warned him that Mrs. Lovell and Mayor Lovell didn't shy away from controversy. They spoke up if the federal government's policies didn't align with their personal preferences for how the island residents should live and work among the animal populations. The last thing Asher wanted was to get into a policy debate with the mayor's wife.

"It's a real shame what happened." Mrs. Lovell's brow puckered as she patted his arm. "We're glad you've come home to regroup."

Wait. What? "Excuse me?"

"Your wife leaving you and all." She lowered her voice and leaned closer. "Mr. Lovell and I are keeping you in our prayers."

"But—"

"C'mon, sweetie." His mother swooped in, linked her arm through his and tugged him away from the conversation. "Let's get Cameron. You don't want to keep those precious volunteers waiting."

Asher disconnected his arm from hers. "What are you doing?"

"Thwarting your demise," she said through gritted teeth. "Sarah Lovell is a nosy gossip. The less information you feed her, the better off you'll be."

Asher barked out a laugh, which only drew more curious stares from the other adults moving through the corridor. "Maybe I wouldn't be in this position if you hadn't fed her false information."

His mother's steps faltered, but she kept her fake smile plastered in place. "I told you, I was only trying to help."

"Lying isn't helpful." Asher dipped his head low to keep their conversation private. Well, as private as possible in a crowded church on Sunday morning. "People are believing things that aren't true about a person who doesn't exist."

Mom stopped and faced him, her brow crimped. "Do you really want them to know the truth?"

He tunneled his fingers through his hair and glimpsed Tess and her sister Rylee walking toward them. "Not yet."

"Not ever." Mom's eyes welled with unshed tears. "Trust me. These people don't really want the truth. I've already lost my marriage and two of my children. I refuse to lose you and Cameron, too."

Her words landed like a fist in his gut. Before he could respond, she swung her oversize leather handbag over her shoulder, then pushed through the crowd without looking back.

Lost her marriage and two of her children? Her chilling words made his scalp prickle. What did that mean? Sure, his brother, Justin, and Krista lived in other states, but they weren't estranged. Were they? The weight of Tess's eyes on him tugged his gaze to meet hers. Something undecipherable flickered in her features before she turned away and spoke to a young couple Asher didn't recognize.

"Dad, come get me." Cameron's words pulled his attention back to the task at hand. Cameron stood in the doorway of the second-and-third-grade classroom, his elbows propped on the half door dividing the room from the corridor.

"Hey, pal." Asher made his mouth form a smile. "How was your class?"

"Super boring." Cameron hopped up and down. "Can we get pizza?"

Asher flashed the volunteer an apologetic glance. "Sorry."

"No problem." The young woman shrugged, then removed the sticker from the back of Cameron's sweater. "He did great. If you'll show me your sticker and they match, he'll be free to go."

"Oh, right." Asher pulled the stub from his pants pocket and gave it to her.

She double-checked the numbers, then released the door. "See you next week, Cameron."

Cameron slid through the opening, then skipped down the hallway, dodging past families with small children. He mowed over a little girl half his size and kept right on going.

"Cam, wait," Asher called after him, trying to keep up as his son rushed toward the door. The little girl burst into tears and the woman beside her glared at Asher.

"I'm sorry." Asher stooped and helped her to her feet. Her cries resounded in the hallway. Great. Add knocking over small children to the list of reasons why people were probably talking about him and Cameron. Wailing, the girl ran into her mother's outstretched arms.

"It's fine. Really." The woman frowned, picked up her daughter and shot Asher another fierce glare before walking away.

Apparently not fine. He sighed, then turned and hurried toward the door. Cameron couldn't be trusted once he broke free of the building's confines. Despite multiple warnings about darting between vehicles in parking lots, he wasn't confident Cameron would remember.

"Dad, look." Cameron stood near the exit, smiling up at Tess. "I found Miss Test. Can she get pizza with us?"

* * *

Absolutely not.

Tess shot Asher a look, silently imploring him to say no.

"That sounds fun." Rylee whipped out her phone. "My friend Abby's the hostess at The Tide Pool. I'll get her to save us a table."

Tess's hand shot out and covered the screen. "Wait."

Rylee's dark eyebrows sailed upward. "What's wrong?"

"I thought we were going to see Grandmother today?"

Their grandmother lived alone in a remote part of the island in a cabin her late husband had built. Rylee often flew out to visit her and had offered to bring Tess along.

"The weather isn't cooperating. Low visibility." Rylee gestured toward the gray skies outside the church. "I can't fly in this."

Drat. "I'm sure Asher and Cameron have plenty of other people to eat lunch with." She forced her mouth into a smile and glanced at Asher. There. She'd given him an out. The perfect opportunity to redirect Cameron and save them all the agony of sharing a meal together.

"No, we don't." Cameron frowned. "My grammie left."

"Asher?" Rylee prompted, her fingers still hovering over her phone.

He raked his hand through his hair. "Yeah, sure. Grab us a table. The more the merrier, right?"

His weak smile did nothing to settle the churning in her abdomen. *Why in the world didn't he say no?*

That didn't mean she couldn't. If her sister thought this was such a wonderful idea, then she could go alone.

"Yahoo!" Cameron thrust both arms in the air like he'd caught the biggest fish in the annual prize-winning salmon derby. "C'mon, guys."

"Whoa, Cam," Asher called out. "You need to hold my hand."

Tess stepped into Cameron's path and blocked him from leaving. "Let's wait for your dad, buddy. That parking lot's busy."

Cameron stared up at her. His dark eyes widened. She braced for him to ignore her instruction and dash for the door anyway. Instead, he flashed her an adorable grin. "Can I sit by you at lunch, Miss Test?"

Her breath caught. How could she say no to such a sweet request? Or correct his adorable mispronunciation of her name? His gap-toothed smile reminded her so much of her brother, Charlie. She glanced at Rylee, but her sister was too absorbed in her phone to notice. Probably working on securing that table. Sorrow swooped in like a bald eagle, its sharp talons clawing at her heart. *Oh, Charlie. We miss you so much.*

"Can I?" Cameron tugged on her sleeve.

Tess nodded. "Of course."

Asher moved toward her, his brow furrowed. She spun away, determined to keep as much space between them as possible. He knew her too well and she did not want to talk about this rogue wave of emotion threatening to take her down. Besides, the gray-blue color of his puffy down jacket transformed his eyes into a shade of velvety blue. She was so enamored with the color that she could hardly stand to look at him without blushing.

"Done." Rylee pocketed her phone and flashed a triumphant smile. "Abby's holding a table for four."

"Great." Asher steered Cameron out the door. "We'll meet you there."

"See you soon." Rylee's car keys jangled as she pulled them from her purse and followed Asher and Cameron outside.

Wait. Tess trudged after her. She wasn't ready. Tutoring Cameron alone in her classroom was so much easier than sharing a meal with Asher.

"Later, gator." Cameron bounded across the asphalt like a kangaroo. Asher reached out and gently clasped his shoulder before he ran between two minivans parked in front of the building.

Wow, the kid was quick. Impulsive, too.

The wind picked up and swirled around them, blowing rain against her cheeks. Tess shivered, then lifted the hood on her jacket and hurried toward Rylee's gray sedan. Her sister was right. The weather wasn't ideal for flying. They'd have to go soon, though. Grandmother took great pride in her self-sufficiency, but Tess needed to see with her own eyes that the cabin was prepared for winter. Charlie's death had made her acutely aware of how much she loved her family. Besides, they'd begged Grandmother every fall to move into Hearts Bay and live in the guesthouse Charlie had started building for her before he'd passed away. The elderly woman had stubbornly refused, but Tess hoped this was the year she'd say yes. Dad could have the cottage on their property fixed up in no time.

"Why are you being so weird?" Rylee slid into the driver's seat, then slammed her door.

"I'm not being weird."

"Oh, you are most definitely being weird." Rylee turned the key in the ignition. "What's wrong?"

Tess blew out a long breath. "He's so—"

"Handsome?"

"What?" Tess reached across the console and nudged Rylee's shoulder. "Stop."

"Oh, please. It's obvious. Every woman with a pulse noticed. Plus, he's got that whole single-dad thing going on."

"What single-dad *thing*?"

Rylee swiveled in the driver's seat to check behind her before shifting into Reverse.

And who was staring at him? She felt strangely possessive of Asher. *So ridiculous.* She reached into her brown leather purse and pulled out her favorite tube of lipstick.

"Relax, all right? I'm not here to steal your man," Rylee said. "This is just lunch. What's the big deal?"

Tess frowned. The big deal? She'd loved Asher with her whole heart. How was she supposed to go back to having lunch and pretending to be his friend?

"And what's with the lipstick?"

She dropped the tube back in her purse, then shoved her bag to the floorboards. "This is hard being back here. If I'd known Asher was…" She trailed off, realizing too late that her comment might hurt her sister's feelings.

Rylee's glare bore into the side of her face. "If you'd known he was here, then what? You wouldn't have moved back?"

"That's not what I was going to say."

A steady rain pelted the windshield as Rylee pulled out of the church parking lot and headed toward the restaurant a few blocks away. "Look, I get it. You guys have a history, but that doesn't mean you can't both live here. Enjoy life. Have lunch together after church. C'mon, Tess. Be a grown-up."

Her sister's words stung. "It's not that simple. He has a kid. Cameron is a painful reminder of the life I said I didn't want. I think it's perfectly normal for me to call the moment and say it's difficult for us to spend time together and pretend like thinking about our past doesn't still hurt."

Rylee slowed behind a truck creeping along the street. "Do you want me to drop you off at home?"

Yes.

"No." Tess fisted her hands in her lap. "I can behave like a grown-up and have lunch with my ex."

But after today, no more casual lunches after church. Or dinners, either. She needed a project. Or a new hobby. Something to occupy her free time and her thoughts. Because focusing on Asher and Cameron only reminded her of what she'd given up. And what she didn't have—a family of her own.

He had to tell her. He couldn't keep living a lie.

Asher fidgeted with his napkin-wrapped silverware. Tess and Cameron sat on the other side of the worn wooden table, their heads bent over the coloring pages that doubled as place mats. Beside him, Rylee studied the flier she'd picked up from the rack inside the door of The Tide Pool. Based on the orange-and-yellow color scheme and the pumpkin graphic in the corner, he figured it was an advertisement for next month's fall festival. She hummed softly, her head bobbing side to side in rhythm to the familiar pop song playing over the speaker in the ceiling.

What he wouldn't give for even a fraction of her

positive attitude. She'd always been a leap-first, ask-questions-later kind of girl. Probably because she wasn't trying to conceal a scandalous secret.

Asher swiped his clammy palms on his pants. He took pride in staying the course when it came to doing the right thing. But how was he supposed to tell Tess that the adoption she'd signed off on had never actually happened?

"Dad, look. Miss Test drew a boat." Cameron's excitement made Tess smile. The light in her dark eyes sent him careening back in time to countless meals and slices of pizza shared at this same restaurant. Guilt slinked in, reminding him that his son had a right to know his mother.

"I see that." Asher forced out the words. "Nice work."

Her gaze held his long enough to make his pulse speed up, then she looked back at her drawing. Her attention returned to Cameron. "This picture needs some fish. Or maybe a whale. What do you think?"

Cameron nodded and reached for the gray crayon from the plastic cup in the middle of the table. "I can draw a whale. Watch."

Cameron poked his tongue into the corner of his mouth and started adding to the drawing on the piece of paper he shared with Tess. Her dark hair spilled forward as she angled her head to one side and watched Cameron work.

Asher had to look away. Mother and son coloring together did a number on his heart. He rolled his neck from side to side, then pulled in a deep breath. They were having lunch. Not a big deal. Coloring and eating pizza wasn't that much different from their weekly tutoring sessions, right?

The silent debate made his frazzled nerves hum. He reached for his soda and took a long sip. Rylee shot him a curious glance. What if he broke the news right here? Just blurted out the truth? Tess had her sister here for moral support. Someone to drive her home if she got upset.

He set his glass down, then scanned the restaurant for their server. She'd taken their order already and probably wouldn't be back with the food for a few minutes. He had time.

The words died on his lips, though. Blindsiding Tess wasn't fair. And part of him worried how her response would affect Cameron. She'd made her feelings abundantly clear—she didn't want a child. This was the kind of news he should share when they were alone, instead of in the middle of a crowded restaurant. Or in front of their son.

His phone rang, buzzing against the table. He hesitated, then glanced at the screen. *Krista.* They'd tried to connect a few times this week but had missed each other's calls every time. She'd be able to give him some guidance about Cameron's reading challenges, so he hated to let it go to voice mail. But part of him didn't want to miss the opportunity to talk to Tess and Rylee.

"Go ahead." Rylee nudged his shoulder with hers. "We've got this."

Asher shook his head and declined the call.

"It's no problem." Tess offered him a reassuring smile. "We can hang with Cameron."

His phone hummed again. A new text message from Krista popped up.

Answer your phone. This is an emergency. Mom's in an ambulance on her way to the hospital.

"Oh no." Asher grabbed his phone and shoved back his chair. "My mom is on her way to the hospital. I've got to go."

"Grammie?" Cameron looked up, his eyes wide. "Is she okay?"

"I—I don't know." Asher swallowed past the tightness in his throat and shrugged into his jacket. "Hope so."

"Go on," Tess said. "We'll take care of him."

"Are you sure? It might be a while."

"We'll go to our parents' house after lunch," Rylee said, her voice calm. Upbeat. "It will be fun."

Asher paused, images from the countless hours he'd spent at the Maddens' beautiful home flooding his mind. He had tremendous respect for Mr. and Mrs. Madden. They had no idea Cameron was their grandson. Mentally, he added their names to the growing list of people who'd be hurt and angry when they uncovered the truth.

"Thanks." He choked out the word. "I'll keep you posted."

Tess's eyes found his. "We're praying."

Regret pierced him. Her kindness served up another reminder that she deserved the truth. For now, all he could manage was a quick nod. He skirted the corner of the table and kissed the top of Cameron's head. "Be good, pal. I'll pick you up as soon as I can."

"'Kay." Cameron kept the gray crayon moving, a gray whale taking shape on the coloring page.

Asher hurried from the restaurant and jogged toward his truck parked across the street. The sharp fishy scent that permeated the air near the waterfront floated on the cool breeze. A lanyard clanked on a boat's mast moored in the harbor. If only his recent conversation with Mom hadn't taken such an unfortunate turn. He wished he'd gone after her instead of letting her leave the church. And he wished Krista, Justin and Dad weren't so far away. A medical emergency wasn't something he wanted to navigate on his own.

A few minutes later, he pulled into the parking lot at Orca Island Community Hospital, then raced into the emergency room. The doors slid shut behind him with a whoosh and he almost collided with Tess's older sister, Mia.

"Asher." She stepped back, a groove forming on her smooth brow. "Are you all right?"

"My mom." His chest rose and fell as he tried to catch his breath. "I got a text that she came here in an ambulance."

Without waiting for Mia to respond, he craned his neck to see past her. Across the waiting room, a young red-haired woman wearing black scrubs sat in an alcove behind a sliding glass window.

"I'm sorry to hear that," Mia said. "Let me see if I can help. Come with me."

So Mia Madden had a job in health care. Good for her. She'd always talked about it, but he wasn't sure how things had worked out. Then again, after he'd left the island with Cameron, he'd avoided any updates. Especially about Tess. Other than Charlie's death last year, he'd intentionally stayed out of the loop regarding any news about the Madden family.

"I have a text that says a neighbor found my mom unresponsive." His loafers squeaked on the gray linoleum floor as he followed Mia across the crowded waiting area. An older man sat in one of the blue vinyl chairs with a bloodstained towel wrapped around his hand. A blonde woman stood near the windows, swaying side to side with a wailing baby braced against her shoulder.

"I'm only here because I brought a friend in." Mia's words pulled Asher's attention back to the woman at the admitting desk. "Even though I'm off today, I can probably help you find out what's going on."

The window slid open. A badge clipped to the redhead's lapel showed her name was Brenda. "Hi, Mia. May I help you?"

"Hi, Brenda." Mia smiled. "This is Asher Hale. His mother came in a little while ago. Can you give us an update, please?"

Brenda's green eyes shifted to Asher. "I'll need to see your ID first, please."

Asher nodded, then pulled his wallet from his pocket and showed her his driver's license.

"Thank you." Brenda tucked a loose curl behind her ear, then jiggled the mouse on her computer. "Give me one second."

Asher jangled his car keys in his pocket and tamped down the urge to turn and push through the doors leading to the triage area. He couldn't, of course. The bright yellow-and-black signs posted on the wall declared the area off-limits. He blew out an impatient breath, earning him a sympathetic glance from Mia and a pointed stare from Brenda.

"They've already admitted her," Brenda said. "Second floor, room two twenty-five."

"Thanks," Mia said. "Dr. Baldwin is the attending physician?"

"He's on until seven."

Mia turned from the window. "Why don't I walk upstairs with you and help find your mother's room. We might cross paths with Dr. Baldwin and get more information."

Asher could only nod and follow her toward the elevator nearby. He wasn't sure what he'd done to deserve this version of Mia. Her kind demeanor and willingness to help was a far cry from the booth full of Madden women he'd encountered at the café his first week back in town.

He only hoped she'd respond with the same grace and kindness when she found out that Cameron was her nephew.

"Miss Test, watch me."

Cameron flung another stone into the choppy water slapping against the rocky coastline edging her parents' property.

"I'm watching." Tess shivered, then zipped up her jacket to her chin. "Nice throw."

The rain had stopped and late afternoon sunlight spilled from the clouds overhead. Fresh snow dusted the tips of the mountains across the inlet. Winter wasn't far away. She stamped her feet to keep warm and jammed her hands deeper into her pockets. Cameron had begged to come outside. They'd already played two rounds of Uno, helped Mom make brownies and he'd listened while she'd read him a children's book, so she couldn't bring herself to say no to some fresh air. Besides, the damp chill in the air didn't seem to bother Cameron.

Her phone buzzed. Even though she'd expected

Asher's message, the sight of his name and his text filling the bubble on her screen made her breath catch.

They've admitted Mom. She's staying the night. I can pick up Cameron in 30 minutes. Where should I meet you?

She asked him to come to her parents' house, then put her phone away. Cameron's proximity to the water required her full attention.

"Cameron, your dad will be here in about thirty minutes."

"Aw, man." He flung another stone into the frothy gray-green water. "Can I stay longer? Please?"

Her heart squeezed. "I'm glad you like it here. This is one of my favorite spots, too. I'm sure your dad will want to get home. You have school tomorrow, remember?"

"But I don't want to go yet," he said. "I'm going to ask if he'll throw rocks with me."

She couldn't help but smile. This was where she and Asher used to spend hours tossing stones into the water, building structures out of driftwood and playing tag in her parents' enormous yard.

Now, all these years later, she'd spent the afternoon babysitting his son. Rylee had conveniently been called into work to cover for another pilot who had the flu. Tess had panicked at first. What if Cameron got bored or upset about his grandmother's condition? The time had flown by, though, and he'd only asked for an update once.

Part of her felt silly for worrying about how to keep a seven-year-old occupied when she spent her days with an entire classroom full of second-graders. But Cameron wasn't just a student. If she was honest, hanging out with him forced her to grapple with her past. So many complicated feelings rose to the surface whenever she thought about Cameron and Asher.

Especially Asher.

Five months into her pregnancy, when she couldn't hide her round abdomen under a bulky sweatshirt any longer, she'd told him she'd never wanted to be a mother. That night marked the first of many arguments about her desire to establish an adoption plan. Every time she brought up the topic, Asher had said he didn't believe her. Insisted that she'd be a wonderful mother and their families would help them every step of the way. To be honest, she hadn't wanted to be a mother at nineteen.

But now she'd love to be a mother. And seeing Asher with Cameron made her question her decision all over again.

What if she'd rejected the best person she'd ever known? Maybe the only man she'd ever love?

She squeezed her eyes shut and battled back the memory of their final argument before she went into labor. Before their harsh words had shredded the remnants of their tattered relationship.

This baby ruined my life!

Her breath hitched as those terrible words repeated in her head. She'd never forget the horrified look in Asher's eyes. Worse, she'd flung a vase across the room. When it shattered against the wall, her parents came running. Dad had firmly escorted Asher out the door.

That was the last time she saw him.

"Miss Test, are you sleeping?"

Cameron's question yanked her back to the present. She opened her eyes and plastered a smile on her face. He stood in front of her, holding the hollow shell of a crab.

"Nope. Just thinking."

"You close your eyes to think?" He wrinkled his adorable little nose. "That's weird."

She laughed. "I appreciate your honesty. What did you find?"

"A crab." He grinned, waving his treasure in the air. The crab's remaining legs wiggled.

"I know some fun facts about crabs," she said. "Are you ready?"

"You know about crabs?"

"Of course. I grew up playing out here, just like you are right now."

"Okay, tell me." He cocked his head to one side in a gesture so reminiscent of Asher that she couldn't help but stare.

"They can live to be thirty years old, weigh as much as twenty pounds and travel up to a mile a day. Here's my favorite fact—their blood is *blue*."

"No way." Cameron's eyes widened. "You're joking."

"Nope." She propped her fists on her hips, superhero style. "All my fun facts are true. Always and forever."

"Cool." He dropped the crab into the water lapping nearby and ran off in the direction of his driftwood collection. "Be right back."

She watched him go, breathing a sigh of relief that he had asked no questions about mama crabs and their babies. Asher would not be pleased if he had to have an awkward conversation about that. Her heart pinched, thinking about the woman who gave birth to this precious boy and all that she was missing by not being in his life.

She shook off the thought before it led to even more reflection and reminiscing about her own child and all that she'd missed by choosing not to be a part of his life. Quickening her steps, she followed Cameron, determined to stiff-arm those painful thoughts. She'd tried to do the right thing for her baby. Asher insisted that they could handle parenthood, but she'd clung to her stubborn belief that teenagers weren't prepared to raise a child. They were still kids themselves.

One fact she couldn't ignore—Rylee had been right about Asher. He did in fact have that whole single-dad thing going on and it was quite attractive. Raised all kinds of warning flags, too. She couldn't be this close to him. Not again. Their breakup had wrecked her. Sure, she'd dated when she was in college and graduate school. Last year, she'd met a teacher at a high school in Fairbanks and thought for sure he was The One. But when it came time to make a serious commitment, she hadn't been able to follow through. They broke up shortly before she moved back to the island. The sense of relief she'd felt had bothered her. Scared her just a little.

Because what if she never could move on? It wasn't fair that Asher still held that special place in her heart.

She'd help Cameron. Keep him safe, care for him during his family emergency and help him improve his reading because it wasn't right to be selfish and put her own needs first. But as soon as Asher's mother's condition improved, she'd resume her role as the teacher across the hall and Cameron's tutor. Nothing more.

Chapter Five

He hadn't been back here in years. Not since the day before Tess delivered Cameron.

Asher parked his truck in front of the Maddens' white two-story house and turned off the engine. The orange-and-gold floral wreath mounted on the front door reminded him of all the times he'd lingered outside with Tess, soaking up the last minutes before her curfew, until her father flashed the porch light. A silent warning that it was time for him to leave. Movement along the shoreline caught his attention and saved him from more reminiscing.

Cameron's yellow hooded sweatshirt and red puffy vest stood out against the gray-blue backdrop of the ocean and the mountains shaped like a sleeping lady across the inlet. He flung a rock into the water, then turned and looked up at Tess. Although he couldn't hear their conversation, the happiness reflected in Cam's expression confirmed what he'd suspected since he'd picked up Cameron from their first tutoring session.

They were bonding.

The realization drove a spike of regret straight

through him. He had to tell her the truth. And use a method of delivery that didn't make her hate him forever.

He climbed out of the truck and slammed the door. Tess glanced his way and waggled her fingertips. She paired her casual wave with a half smile that made his pulse accelerate.

Perfect. His brain had evidently failed to notify his heart that their romance didn't stand a second chance. *He* didn't deserve a second chance. His family had obliterated any hope of reconciliation when they'd faked the adoption.

Cameron scooped another stone from the ground and tossed it into the water. He hadn't acknowledged Asher yet. Probably pretending not to notice him so he didn't have to stop throwing things and go home. He couldn't fault him for that. Playing out here, especially with Tess, had been one of his favorite childhood adventures, too.

The buzz of a saw somewhere nearby overpowered Cameron's chatter. Asher glanced behind the Maddens' house. A cottage sat nestled in the trees at the back of their property. Two sawhorses stood in front, supporting a sheet of plywood. Sawdust fluttered in the air as Mr. Madden cut through the board.

Asher quickly averted his gaze. He wasn't ready to look the man in the eye. Even though seven years had passed, they hadn't parted on good terms.

"Hey." Tess's dark eyes searched his face as he joined her. "How's your mom?"

"She's resting comfortably. Proud owner of a hot pink cast on her arm."

"Oh no." Tess scrunched her nose. "I'm sorry to hear that."

"Thanks. It could've been so much worse. They're keeping her overnight to monitor her blood sugar. Hopefully she can go home tomorrow." Asher shoved his hands into his jacket pockets. "How did things go with Cameron?"

Tess followed Asher's gaze. Cameron scampered down the beach to inspect a piece of driftwood. Asher couldn't stop a smile. Yet another reminder of his and Tess's many adventures out here.

"He's been fun to have around."

Asher studied her. The wistful tone in her voice was impossible to miss. His chest tightened with a pang of regret. The day before she'd gone into labor, she'd insisted that she never wanted to be a mother. He'd called her a liar. It wasn't a moment he was proud of, especially since she'd have every right to accuse him of the same. Did she ever think about the past? And how her choices affected him? And when she found out that Cameron was her son, would she still want to be around them?

Tess faced him. Any trace of regret or wistfulness had vanished. "It's none of my business, really, but if you don't mind my asking, what happened to your mother?"

He blew out a long breath. For a second, he'd feared this was the moment she confronted him about Cameron's mother. If she asked him directly, he'd have to tell her everything. "My mom doesn't manage her diabetes very well. She's really stubborn. Some might even say reckless. Neighbors found her unresponsive in the yard today. I can't imagine what might've happened if—"

"Stop." Tess's hand shot out and squeezed his arm. "They found her. That's what matters."

Her touch sent a feeling of warmth up his arm and straight to his chest. An express train of happiness and delight bound for his heart. He glanced at her hand still clasping his jacket sleeve, silently willing her not to pull back once she realized what she'd done. Slowly, he dragged his gaze to meet hers. He remembered how her brown eyes sometimes looked like they held flecks of gold. Even the tiny scar above her left eyebrow was as familiar to him as his own hand. Funny how he once believed that he'd have forever to stare into her beautiful eyes. He couldn't look away. Then something undecipherable flickered across her features and she stuffed her hand deep in her pocket.

No!

He rubbed his mouth with his fingertips, determined to keep the protest from slipping out. Oh, how he wanted to pull her into his arms. The ache to hold her close and rest his cheek against her silky hair was almost unbearable.

"Daddy!" Cameron barreled toward them, puncturing the moment. Tess stepped farther away as Cameron crashed into Asher and flung his arms around his waist.

"Hey, pal." Asher hugged the little boy close and exchanged smiles with Tess. "Having fun?"

"Is my grammie okay?" Cameron pulled back and swiped his coat sleeve across his nose.

Gross. Asher grimaced. "She has to spend the night at the hospital, but she can come home tomorrow if the doctor says it's okay."

"Oh, dear." Tess produced a tissue. "Here you go."

Cameron shook his head and ran off. "Let's throw more rocks, Daddy."

"You may throw five more and then we're going home. Miss Tess needs some me time."

"Me time?" Cameron's belly laugh bubbled into the crisp air. "What's that mean?"

"It means she gave up her entire afternoon for you. Now we need to go home and leave her alone," Asher said.

"She's not alone." Cameron kneeled and collected a handful of small stones. "Her daddy's right over there. What's he making, anyway?"

Tess turned and glanced toward the cottage. "He's finishing up that small house so my grandmother will have a nice place to live this winter."

"Oh, let's go see." Cameron flung his handful of stones into the water all at once, then turned and trotted across the yard.

"Cameron, wait," Asher called, but the kid broke into the seven-year-old version of a sprint.

"Oh, boy." Asher hurried after him. This wasn't how he wanted to say hello to Tess's father.

"It's fine." Tess caught up. "Dad will be happy to show him around."

"But he won't be happy to see me."

Tess shot him a look. "We're all adults here, Asher. That was a long time ago."

"Tess, I need to—"

"No, you don't." Her expression hardened. "It's been a rough day. Let's not go there right now."

His heart hammered. But Cameron was about to meet his grandfather. Shouldn't he say something?

"I mean it, Asher." Tess stopped walking and faced him. "Moving Grandmother in from her village was all Charlie's idea. He always worried about her. My dad is finishing this house because it was something Charlie started."

She bit her lip. Was she about to cry?

Asher palmed the back of his neck. All right. This was fragile territory. She didn't want to make a hard situation more difficult. "I get it."

"Good."

Tess started walking toward her father, who'd turned off his power tool and stood beside the sawhorse, chatting with Cameron. When they bumped fists, Asher's legs grew weak. Maybe Tess was right. Maybe he should leave the past where it belonged. If she never wanted to be a mother, what good could come from knowing that Cameron was her son? It was certainly easier to abide by her request not to mention their history. Still, he couldn't shake the guilt. Or the ominous feeling that he hadn't fully experienced the fallout of the rumors his mother had spread.

"A booth at the festival?" Eliana frowned. "Are you sure?"

"Of course I'm sure." Rylee flopped on the red sofa beside her. "Our family always sponsors a booth."

"You mean we always sponsored a booth when Charlie was alive." Eliana's voice was barely above a whisper. "We skipped it last year."

Tess shifted in the leather recliner—Charlie's favorite chair—and cradled her teacup and saucer in her lap. Flames crackled in the fireplace beside her. There were two topics she'd hoped to avoid tonight: Charlie's death and Asher Hale.

Since their conversation yesterday outside her parents' house, she hadn't been able to stop thinking about him.

Despite her best efforts to ignore their history together, sweet memories invaded at the most inopportune time. Today her thoughts wandered during a staff meeting and she missed half of the principal's instructions. Then during recess, when she was supposed to be supervising the whole playground, she caught herself watching Cameron play tetherball instead.

"Earth to Tess." Eliana waggled her fingers in the air. "What do you think we should do?"

Busted. Tess sipped her tea, stalling, while she tried to come up with an answer that didn't reveal her mind had wandered. Again.

"She's not paying attention." Rylee's eyes gleamed as she propped her feet on the wood-and-metal table. Tiny navy blue airplanes adorned her pale blue socks. "Too busy thinking about Asher."

Tess's teacup clattered against the saucer. "I agree with Eliana. I don't think I'm up for hosting a booth at the festival."

"Wow, okay." Rylee's expression grew serious. "Didn't realize I was hanging with a bunch of Debbie Downers tonight. I thought it would be a nice way to honor Charlie's memory. The fall festival was one of his favorite activities in Hearts Bay."

"I know." Eliana sighed and burrowed deeper under the yellow blanket spread across her lap. "But hosting a booth without him makes me sad."

"We're going to have to move on, El." Rylee shot Tess a help-me-out-here look. "He wouldn't want us to sit around being sad."

Ouch. Tess winced as Eliana's chin wobbled. Not everyone shared Rylee's philosophy. Before she could respond, the front door opened and Mia swept in. Pink tinged her cheeks, and a frigid breeze swirled in behind her.

"Sorry I'm late." She nudged the door closed with her shoulder, then held up a covered pan. "Maybe cheesecake will atone for my tardiness."

"Only if it's pumpkin cheesecake." Rylee scooted over on the sofa to make space for Mia. "Did you make that yourself?"

Mia nodded and toed off her sneakers. "I've started baking to keep myself occupied."

Tess bit her lip. Here she sat, feeling sorry for herself because she couldn't stop thinking about Asher, but Mia had lost Charlie *and* her fiancé. Somehow she'd kept moving forward, despite the horrific losses in her life. Tess had to find a way to do the same.

"I'll get plates and forks." Eliana shoved the blanket aside and stood. "Mia, do you want something to drink?"

"Decaf coffee, please." Mia set the cheesecake on the coffee table. "What did I miss?"

"We're talking about hosting a booth at the fall festival," Rylee said. "Do you have your October work schedule?"

"Not yet." Mia shrugged out of her coat, then stood in front of the fireplace, warming her hands. "I haven't been to the festival in years. Did you pick a booth?"

"Funny you should ask." Rylee wound the fringe of Eliana's blanket around her finger. "We're a house divided. I'm in, but Eliana and Tess don't want to get involved."

"That's not what I said," Eliana called from the kitchen. "Don't twist my words."

"She's sad because Charlie's not here," Tess explained.

"What about you, Tess?" Mia asked. "Or are you already helping with a booth for the school?"

Tess hesitated. How could she explain that spending time with kids, especially in a festive setting like the annual fall celebration, filled her with a desperate longing to be a mother? Working with kids all day in her classroom didn't bother her. She could separate her job from her painful past. But any time she saw families together—the church hallway or even lunch at The Tide Pool—it felt like salt poured in an open wound.

But this wasn't about her.

They were honoring Charlie's memory. So she swallowed her heartache and plastered on a smile. "A booth would be a nice way to give back to the community and honor Charlie's memory at the same time."

"Exactly." Rylee pumped her fist in the air. "Mia? Are you in?"

Eliana returned with a pie server, plates and forks. She set them on the table beside the cheesecake, then pried off the plastic lid.

"How about that fishing game? Mom still has the plastic poles and the fish with the magnets stored in her garage," Mia said. "I saw the boxes when I was digging around in there last week."

"What were you digging in their garage for?" Eliana paused, a slice of cheesecake suspended over a plate.

A look that could only be described as panic flashed across Mia's face, then quickly vanished.

"Nothing. It's—never mind." Mia slid an elastic band from her wrist and twisted her hair into a messy bun.

"Let's choose our theme for the booth before we're left with only the crummy stuff."

Eliana and Tess exchanged glances. This wasn't the first time Mia's exterior had cracked. And not the first time she'd quickly brushed off their questions, either.

"Good point." Rylee held up the crumpled list she'd printed from her email. "The deadline to choose a carnival game is the day after tomorrow. If we decide tonight, I'll text Mrs. Johnson and claim our first choice. She's the festival coordinator this year."

Tess stood and set her cup and saucer on the side table, then helped herself to a slice of cheesecake.

"We should have an alternate idea, too," Mia said. "Since we didn't take part last year, someone else might already have the fishing game in mind."

"Uh-oh." Rylee paused and scanned her phone. "This might be a deal breaker."

Tess reclaimed her spot in the leather recliner and waited for Rylee to explain, silently hoping other groups had already claimed all the booths so they wouldn't have to participate.

You're being ridiculous.

Was she? Was it so ridiculous to waffle between confident she could move on and petrified that she'd never be able to escape her past?

"Come on, don't leave us hanging," Eliana said.

"So I'm sure you've all heard Mrs. Hale fell and broke her arm—"

"Oh no." Tess groaned. "I know exactly where you're headed with this."

"Wait. Let me guess." Eliana held up her palm. "She wants us to run her booth for her."

"Not just any booth," Rylee said. "She already had

dibs on the game with the fish and fishing poles. Mrs. Johnson wants to know if we'll take over for her."

"Is she going to be there?" Tess asked. Had she roped Asher and Cameron into helping her? Talk about a deal breaker. Starting now, she needed to limit how much time she spent with those two outside of school.

"I'd say that's a *no* based on what I've heard from people in the café. She's in terrible shape," Eliana said.

Oh, dear. Tess focused on her cheesecake so her sisters wouldn't see her facial expression. They could always read her so well. If Mrs. Hale struggled with her recovery, that meant more stress on Asher. And less time for him to focus on Cameron's needs if he had to worry about his mother, too.

Rylee's phone chimed with another text message. "Here's the good news. Mrs. Hale already ordered the goldfish we'll need for prizes at the booth, so we don't have to worry about that."

"I like the fishing booth," Mia said. "We're a family of fishermen, after all. Charlie would most definitely approve."

Eliana offered a weak smile. "Then let's do it. For Charlie."

"It's only one night," Tess said. "We can handle it."

Uncertainty filled Rylee's eyes. "Are you sure?"

Another unwelcome image of Cameron tossing a stone into the water and Asher smiling at her flickered in her mind.

Nope. "Absolutely."

"All right, I'm telling the coordinator that we're in and we will team up with Mrs. Hale." Rylee's fingers flew over her phone as she composed the text message.

Forks clinked against their plates as the girls finished

their dessert. Tess tried to ignore the hollow ache settling in her chest.

"I hope Mrs. Hale hires some help. At least temporarily," Mia said. "It's hard to drive or get dressed with a broken arm."

"And she'll have a tough time working," Eliana added, moving toward the kitchen as the coffee maker gurgled and hissed. "How can a travel agent book vacations if she can't type?"

Tess squirmed as Mia and Rylee trained their curious gazes on her. "Why are you looking at me?"

"We thought you might know what's going on since you're Cameron's new tutor," Rylee said, flattening the graham cracker crumbs on her plate with the back of her fork.

"Oh, how's that going?" Eliana returned and handed Mia a steaming mug, then reclaimed her spot on the sofa.

"Cameron's doing fine." Tess forced a smile that she hoped masked her concerns. To be honest, Cameron wasn't doing well. At all. It wouldn't take five more weeks of sessions to identify what she already felt certain was true. He needed an evaluation from a child psychologist and a proper diagnosis.

Mia smiled over the rim of her mug. "So you aren't going to add caregiving to your list of noble after-school activities?"

Tess bristled. Mia might've been teasing, but her words landed wrong. "Not for Mrs. Hale. Why would I?"

Surprise flashed in Mia's eyes as she sipped her coffee. Swallowing, she cast a nervous glance toward Eliana and Rylee. "In the past, you've always been the first to jump in and help when someone was struggling."

Except when it really mattered. Her baby had needed her and she'd turned her back. The sound of his newborn cry echoed in her memory. Goose bumps shot down her arms as she recalled the nurse lifting him from the bassinet and carrying him away.

"Tess?" Mia's voice pulled her back to the present. "I'm sorry if I hurt you. I was only teasing."

"It's fine." Tess lifted her chin. *I'm fine.*

"So you're okay with us helping out Mrs. Hale with the booth?" Rylee asked. "Because we can come up with an alternate idea and I can email Mrs. Johnson tonight."

"I don't mind helping with the booth at the festival, but if Mrs. Hale needs a caregiver Asher's going to have to ask somebody else."

Sure, she might've had a reputation for taking in stray animals and fixing meals for people in the community who were recovering from surgery, but this time she wouldn't be the first one in line to volunteer. Because every time she saw Asher and Cameron, they reminded her of what she'd lost. She had to stop allowing her present circumstances to punish her for a past decision she could never change. But how?

"I need your help, Justin." Asher paced the floor in Dad's house between the kitchen and living room. "Mom's a mess."

Justin hesitated. "Give me a minute… No, baby, don't go."

Baby? Asher stuffed down a groan. If Justin had a new girlfriend, the possibility of him agreeing to help decreased by at least half. He and his younger brother hadn't spoken much lately, one of the many casualties of their parents' divorce nine months ago, but the tension had grown by leaps and bounds when Justin had warned him that moving back to Alaska wasn't a wise decision.

"Hang on," Justin said. A door closed in the background. "Okay, sorry about that. What's up?"

"Mom just got out of the hospital. Neighbors found her unresponsive in the driveway shortly after she got home from church. She broke her arm when she fell."

"That stinks."

"Tell me about it."

"Any idea what caused this?"

Asher sank onto the couch. *She's diabetic. Remember?* He battled back the sarcastic response. "Her blood sugar dropped because she skipped breakfast."

"She's always done a lousy job of taking care of herself," Justin scoffed. "I'm sorry this happened, but I'm not surprised."

Asher leaned forward and plucked a crumpled foil candy wrapper hidden under a stack of magazines. Had Cameron been sneaking candy out of the kitchen cabinet? He made a mental note to talk to him in the morning.

"Like I said, I really need your help." Asher sank back against the couch cushions. "Just for a few days. Cameron's having some issues and he might need to see a specialist in Anchorage. I'm going to try and schedule the appointment during his fall break. We might be gone for a few days and I don't want Mom to be here alone."

"I can't drop everything and fly to Alaska. I have a job. Responsibilities. There's—"

"Your new girlfriend. *Baby?*"

"Well, I'd be lying if I said she wasn't influencing my decisions. Did you see the pictures I posted? We spent last weekend at this phenomenal place near San Diego."

"I must've missed those." Asher shook his head. He should've called Krista first. As usual, Justin was clueless. Didn't have time to come and help Mom, but he always had a weekend free to take his girlfriend on a romantic getaway.

"Maybe I could visit during Thanksgiving."

What? Surely he was kidding. "That's two months from now."

"Like I said, I'm slammed right now. Got to meet those quarterly sales targets and all that."

And spend quality time with Baby.

"You do realize she has a broken arm." Asher fought to keep his voice even. "It's her right hand, which is her dominant side. So she's in a cast for six weeks—"

"And milking this for all it's worth." Justin chuckled. "I can only imagine her list of excessive demands."

"She can't get dressed by herself or fix her own meals and she needs help with her insulin. I'd hardly call that excessive."

"Tough love, bro. She's an adult. It's her responsibility to manage her health conditions. If she regulated her blood sugar like she was supposed to, maybe this wouldn't have happened."

Asher pushed his hand through his hair. He couldn't argue with that. But he'd also noticed a connection between their mother's heartache and her behavior. She seemed hurt. Maybe even a little lonely. He wasn't a doctor or a mental health professional, but part of him suspected that she made reckless choices to get attention.

"Did you call Krista?"

"Not yet."

"I think she's your best option."

"Justin—"

"You know I'd like to help."

Justin's excuses mixed with fake empathy grated on Asher's nerves. "Great. Then you'll book a flight?"

"That's not what I said. Look, man, things are hectic at work right now. This isn't a good time for me."

"That's the problem with family emergencies," Asher growled. "They never happen at a convenient time."

"Dude, relax. You'll figure this out."

"Apparently with zero help from you. Thanks for nothing."

He ended the call, then tossed his phone on the couch. Why was Justin being so selfish?

Lord, that did not go well at all. Please help me find someone to stay with Mom.

"Daddy?" Cameron's soft voice wobbled from somewhere behind him. "Are you mad?"

Oh no. Asher stifled a groan. He swiveled on the couch and glanced toward the hallway.

Cameron stood in the kitchen, his hair sticking up. He rubbed a fist over his eye. Poor kid. He looked exhausted.

"I was talking to Uncle Justin, buddy. What are you doing up?"

Guilt pinched his insides. He'd already put Cameron to bed once. Had he really been awake for an entire hour?

"I couldn't sleep and your voice got kind of loud. Did Uncle Justin do something wrong?"

Asher hesitated. Cameron didn't get to see Justin very often. The last thing he wanted was to paint his brother in a negative light. Even though their conversation had made him angry, he still wanted Cameron to look forward to their next visit.

Whenever Justin fit them into his packed schedule.

He pushed to his feet. "Come on, you need to get some sleep. I'll tuck you in."

Cameron yawned and raised his arms in the air. "Carry me."

His heart swelled. Cameron never wanted to be carried anymore. "You got it." He leaned down and scooped his son into his arms. As Cameron snuggled against him, Asher breathed in the familiar smell of apple-scented kids' shampoo and tried to savor the moment. Before long, the kid would be wearing cologne and asking to borrow the car.

He padded down the short hallway and into Cameron's room, then gently lowered him to the mattress on the twin bed. Cameron squirmed around and tugged his green dinosaur-print pajama top down over his matching shorts.

"Are you cozy?" Asher asked.

"More blankets, please."

"Another blanket, coming right up." Asher grabbed the green fleece blanket folded at the bottom of the bed and layered it on top of the comforter Cameron had already tugged to his chin. Asher reached for Sammy the sea otter, Cameron's favorite stuffed animal and most prized possession, and tucked it under the comforter. Sammy once traveled everywhere they went. When Cam started school, he'd agreed to leave Sammy at home during the day, but he always went to sleep with the beloved stuffed animal in his arms.

"There you go." Asher reached over to turn off the lamp on the bedside table.

"Daddy, wait. Will you read to me?"

"It's late, bud. Over an hour past your bedtime."

Cameron's eyebrows scrunched together. "I tried to read it myself, 'cept the words were all squished together so I couldn't."

Asher froze, his arm still extended toward the lamp. *Tried to read but the words were squished together.* He left the lamp on and sank down on the mattress. That was a key piece of information he'd need to share with Mrs. Franklin. And Tess.

Pushing all thoughts of his son's mother aside, he retrieved the book from the floor. "Is it this dinosaur book?"

Cameron nodded. "Read it to me, please? Just one time."

"Sure."

Asher read every page of the story about dinosaurs saying good-night.

After he finished, Cameron yawned again. "I have another question."

"Okay. Hit me."

"What's a...speshliss?"

"A specialist is someone who is very good at their job."

"Are you an animal speshliss?"

"Kind of." Asher closed the book and set it on the nightstand. "Let's talk about this tomorrow."

"I'm a dinosaur speshliss," Cameron mumbled, his eyes slowly closing.

Asher chuckled, then leaned down and kissed his forehead. "That you are. Good night. I love you."

"Love you," Cameron whispered as he burrowed deeper under his comforter.

Two precious words that Cameron rarely uttered. Asher's throat tightened against an unexpected wave of emotion. This kid. What a blessing. Sure, he struggled to parent on his own, but tender moments like this made all the challenges worth it.

And reminded him of all that Tess had missed.

Chapter Six

Dear Lord, please help her land this thing.

Tess dug her nails into her palms and craned her neck to see out her tiny window in the Piper Cub's jump seat. If she'd been standing on the village's flat, safe dock that jutted out into the water like a pointed finger, the bay's beautiful emerald green water might've filled her with awe. But from inside her baby sister's seaplane soaring in the sky, the view only made her queasy.

"I've got this." Rylee's voice crackled in her headphones. "You can stop panicking."

"I'm not panicking."

Much.

Tess forced air into her constricted lungs. Flying made her so anxious. Especially when they landed on water. Sure, she'd flown in small planes before. But this was the first time she'd flown with her baby sister at the controls. Something about that just seemed wrong.

"Grandmother will be so happy to see you." Rylee shot her a bright smile. "Seriously. I know what I'm doing. You can relax."

Tess averted her gaze and stared through the windshield. Pulled in another long breath. That's what she was supposed to do, right? Focus on her breathing. And think positive thoughts. "I trust you."

At least she was trying. She didn't want to be afraid. Really, she didn't. But ever since a terrifying experience in high school when the pilot became disoriented during a blizzard, she'd felt nervous.

"Flying with me beats taking the boat, right?"

Tess managed a weak smile. Rylee had a point. Dad used to bring them to visit their grandparents on his boat. The ride lasted almost two hours each way, often in choppy seas. At least Rylee could get them here in thirty minutes.

Visiting Grandmother's village, a community of colorful houses nestled against the rocky hillside, always felt like a leap back in time. A priceless piece of Orca Island's heritage that never changed much, despite the modern conveniences enjoyed by most people who lived in Hearts Bay. Tess couldn't wait to snack on the smoked salmon and crackers Grandmother would undoubtedly share when they arrived at her house. Or hear another one of her incredible stories about her simple but challenging childhood in this rugged environment. Although Tess hated the flight, her discomfort was worth it, especially if they could convince Grandmother to spend the winter in town.

Rylee landed the plane with a gentle bump and they skimmed across the water. Tess spotted a sleek red seaplane with a white stripe bobbing near the dock.

A man in a red-and-black-plaid flannel stood on the dock beside the plane, unloading canvas bags. "Oh, this should be fun," Rylee said.

"What's wrong?"

"Nothing." Rylee kept her eyes trained on the controls.

"It doesn't sound like nothing." Panic welled and Tess scanned their surroundings. They'd landed, hadn't they? The pontoons had done their job. Right? "Why did you say this would be fun?"

"There's nothing wrong with the plane," Rylee said. "I'm talking about the guy in the plaid flannel."

Tess leaned toward the windshield for a closer look. She gripped the armrests on her bucket seat as Rylee slowed the plane and taxied toward the dock. He was still too far away for her to identify him. "Who is he?"

"His name is Ben and he's a pilot," Rylee said. "We've gone out twice."

Huh. Interesting. Tess studied her. "Is that all you're going to tell me?"

Typical Rylee. Happy to tease and soak up all the details about her sisters' personal lives, but with her own, she conveniently shared little. She and Mia were so similar that way.

Rylee lifted one shoulder. "There's not much to tell. We went out, didn't exactly hit it off. He's not my type."

"I'm sorry to hear that."

"No worries." Rylee chuckled. "Brace yourself, though."

Wait. What?

"He's friendly. I'm sure he'll ask you out. Probably before we fly home."

Oh. Her breath hitched.

Ben turned and faced them as Rylee guided the plane in. He grinned and waved. Tess seized the opportunity to study him more closely. His sandy-blond hair peeked out from under a black knit cap. Tall, athletic build. A pilot. Huh. He was handsome in a rugged, outdoorsy way. She hadn't been out with a guy in weeks and lately she'd elevated avoiding her ex-boyfriend to a world-class sport. Was she ready to date someone new?

"Should I hop out and grab a line or something?" Tess craned her neck to see out the window beside her, but all she saw was water sloshing against the edge of the weathered wooden dock.

"Nope. Sit tight," Rylee said. "Ben will tie us off."

As if on cue, the plane's floats bumped against the dock. Ben grabbed a rope anchored to a metal cleat near him and quickly secured the plane. Tess unbuckled her safety belt, took off her headset, then grabbed her bag and pushed open the door.

"Hi," she said. "You must be Ben."

"Good morning." He grinned. "And who might you be?"

Oh, nice smile. "Tess Madden."

She hesitated, gauging the distance between the cockpit and the dock.

"Would you like some help?" He offered his hand. "I'll catch you."

Clasping her fingers in his, she stepped onto the plane's float, wobbled, then leaped the short distance onto the dock. Ben pulled her close, his gaze locked on hers, as he braced the palm of his other hand on the small of her back. She noted his strong, confident grasp, the salt-tinged air mingling with his outdoorsy scent, and she couldn't help but smile back.

"Nice to meet you, Tess."

"Likewise." She waited for the familiar butterflies in her abdomen to make an appearance. Strange. Nothing. "Rylee has told me so much about you."

His green eyes sparked with amusement. "Uh-oh."

"Only the good stuff." She held on to him a smidge longer than necessary, pretending she hadn't regained her footing on the wobbly dock. "I promise."

Ben squeezed her hand, then let go. She tucked a loose strand of hair behind her ear, her gaze still locked on his. The curiosity in his expression was unmistakable.

What are you doing?

She ignored the cynical thought and slung her tote bag over her shoulder. Nothing wrong with a little flirting. If she was going to move on from Asher, she had to date again.

"Hey, Ben." Rylee climbed out of the plane and hopped down beside Tess. "Thanks for helping us out."

"No problem." He angled his head toward the parking lot. "My buddy's truck is right here. Need a lift to your grandmother's place?"

Tess sensed Rylee's hesitation. Something spurred her to say yes before Rylee refused his offer. "Sounds good to me. I wasn't looking forward to that walk."

Grandmother's home sat near the top of the hill overlooking the village. It was a short but intense climb on a muddy dirt road.

"Are you on a mail run?" Rylee asked, as they followed him toward a white mud-spattered truck parked nearby.

"I'm delivering mail and medication." Ben reached for Tess's bag and she allowed him to carry it. "There are a couple of folks out here who ran out of their blood pressure medication."

A few minutes later, they were piled inside Ben's

vehicle. Rylee had let her ride up front while she sat in the back seat beside a filthy canvas duffel bag.

"Nice truck." Tess settled her bag on her lap, then fastened her seat belt. "Does your buddy live nearby?"

"No. He manages the auto parts store in Hearts Bay. He and his wife just bought a cabin out here that they plan to remodel. He lets me borrow his truck when I'm making deliveries."

"Oh, boy." Rylee chuckled. "I see a lot of supply runs in your future."

Rylee and Ben chatted about their favorite recent trips as he guided the truck up the winding dirt road to Grandmother's cabin. Tess half listened while she silently evaluated him. Sandy-blond hair brushed the collar of his buffalo-check button-down shirt, which he'd layered over a black T-shirt. He wore faded jeans and battered dark brown work boots. A bottle of water and pack of chewing gum filled the center console. Seemed like a nice guy. Polite. Friendly. She'd quiz Rylee later about why she hadn't wanted to date him.

Images of Asher and Cameron filled her head. *Stop.* She did not want to think about Asher.

"It's this one, right?" Ben stopped his truck in front of Grandmother's blue-and-white house at the end of a short driveway. Smoke curled from the chimney and a lamp glowed from the front window.

"Thanks for the ride." She opened the door but didn't get out. "It was great to meet you."

"You, too." Something she couldn't quite decipher flickered across his face. "Text me if you need a ride back to your plane."

"Nope, we've got it covered." Rylee nudged Tess's shoulder, nearly pushing her out of the truck.

"Take it easy." Tess stumbled onto the road, fumbling to keep her bag from spilling its contents.

"Thanks again." Rylee climbed out of the truck. "See you around."

Tess shrugged helplessly, then closed the door. Ben waved and drove off. She watched him go, disappointed that he hadn't asked for her number. Rylee strode toward Grandmother's front door. Tess hurried to catch up. "Man, you blew him off quick. What was that all about?"

"That was you being a shameless flirt and me shutting it down."

"I wasn't a shameless flirt," Tess scoffed.

Rylee stopped walking and whirled around. They nearly collided on the path in front of the cabin.

"Ben's a good guy, Tess." Rylee's eyes flashed. "Don't toy with him."

"We just met." Tess held up her palm in defense. "How am I *toying* with him?"

A muscle in Rylee's jaw twitched. "I've seen the way you and Asher still look at each other, and I saw how Ben looked at you today. He's interested. And it's not fair to drag him into the middle of whatever's going on between you and Asher."

"There's nothing going on between me and Asher."

Rylee opened her mouth, then closed it again.

Tess glared. "You don't believe me, do you?"

Grandmother opened the door. "Oh, my sweet girls." Her leathery skin crinkled and her dark eyes gleamed as she smiled. "Come on in."

Tess stepped into her grandmother's warm embrace. The woman stood less than five feet tall, but she gave the best hugs. Tess closed her eyes and breathed in the familiar scent of a baby lotion her grandmother had worn for ages mixed with the pungent scent of smoke from the wood fire used to heat the small home.

They were here to convince Grandmother to move to Hearts Bay for the winter. This wasn't the time to worry about Ben or Asher or whom she should or shouldn't be dating. Today was about family. Doing what was best to keep the people she loved safe. Protected.

But if Ben asked her out on a date, she'd most definitely say yes.

Asher lived for outdoor adventures, especially when they assisted a wounded animal.

He and his partner, Brian, hiked along the island's coast, in search of a stranded harbor seal. Fishermen had alerted them to the distressed animal hauled out on a rocky outcropping. Rescuing an injured sea creature was usually beyond the scope of their jobs, but the game warden had responded to a call on the east end of the island and the volunteers at the local sea life center indicated they didn't have anyone available to respond. Since Asher and Brian were already close by gathering data on the island's puffin population, their boss had sent them on this unconventional rescue mission.

"Our current location matches the GPS coordinates the fishermen sent us." Brian glanced from his phone to the rocks jutting out into the water. "I don't see anything, though."

"Let's walk a little farther," Asher said. "This fog isn't helping."

The sun had appeared briefly before lunch, then disappeared behind a thick blanket of gray clouds. Fog had gradually rolled in off the water, limiting their visibility. Asher zipped his jacket tighter and turned in a slow circle, searching for any sign of a gray seal. The alarm on his phone rang, reminding him that he had thirty minutes until he was supposed to pick up Cameron from the after-school program at the community center.

He would not make it on time. Pulling his phone from his jacket pocket, he silenced the alarm. Before he could think of someone else to call and ask to get Cameron, movement up ahead caught his attention.

"There." He pointed. "What's that?"

Brian raised his binoculars. "Looks like a seal wrapped in a fishing net."

Asher shoved his phone back in his pocket, then bounded over a gap where gray-blue water sloshed between the rocks. He slipped, then scrambled to stay upright, arms flailing. Whoa. That's all he needed—falling into the frigid ocean or spraining his ankle. Puffs of white air floated in front of his mouth as he caught his breath. The temperature was dropping rapidly.

The seal raised its front flippers and growled. Heeding the warning, Asher stopped and glanced back at Brian.

"We'd better hold off," Asher said.

"I'm going to call the game warden and the Coast Guard station." Brian let his binoculars dangle around his neck, then pulled his phone from his pocket. "We're going to need backup. That's a big seal."

"It might not survive the night." Asher glanced toward the sky. He couldn't see ravens or an eagle circling yet, but they'd show up soon. He gripped the straps of his backpack and studied the seal. The animal's shiny dark eyes met his, its sleek body undulating as it flapped both flippers, then growled again.

Poor thing. The net wrapped around the seal cinched tighter the more the animal squirmed. Asher stared, hating the helpless feeling that washed over him. Surely there was something they could do while they waited for more help to arrive.

While Brian spoke to the warden on the phone, Asher scrolled through his short list of contacts for someone who could pick Cameron up from the after-school program. And possibly feed him dinner, too. If he and Brian had to wait for Fish and Game or the Coast Guard, it might be a long night.

He paused his scrolling at Tess's name. No. He wouldn't ask for her help until he'd exhausted all other options, because he didn't want to need her. Besides, she'd say yes. She always did. And every time he called her, his need for help gave her the opportunity to spend more time with Cameron. Frankly, it made him feel guilty. Guilty for not telling her that Cameron was her son. Guilty for depriving Cameron of the knowledge that Tess was his mother.

But she never wanted to be a mom.

The same tired argument resurfaced in his mind. He was starting to wonder if that was still her position. When he watched her with Cameron, she looked like she was doing exactly what she loved. Worse, throwing her and her son together in situations where she cared for him and met his needs made the whole ugly mess more convoluted.

And made it harder for him to not tell her the truth.

He scrolled past her name and sent a text to the neighbors across the street instead. A long shot, but he had to try. They were friendly and tolerated Cameron's incessant questions when they saw each other outside. Probably not interested in taking care of a second-grader for several hours, though.

He definitely would not ask his mother. She'd keep Cameron alive but there was no telling what she'd feed him or let him watch on TV. Besides, she couldn't drive yet, which would make it difficult for her to get to the community center on time to pick Cameron up.

The neighbor responded immediately.

Wish I could help, but I have quilting club tonight and my husband doesn't babysit.

"Thanks so much," Asher muttered. At least she was honest.

Brian pocketed his phone. "The warden says he'll be about forty minutes or so and he could really use our help transporting the animal to the sea life center."

Oh, boy. Asher massaged his forehead with his fingertips.

"Are you all right?"

No. "Yeah, I'm fine. Trying to find a last-minute babysitter for my son."

"That's tough," Brian said. "I'd say send him to our house, but my wife would kill me. She's got her hands full with a baby and a toddler who has a fever."

"I understand." Asher scrolled back to Tess's number. Visions of Cameron sitting all alone at the community center, panicking when no one came to pick him up, twisted his stomach into a hard knot. What a nightmare. He typed out his desperate plea for help, then sent the text.

Less than a minute later, she responded with a generous offer to pick Cameron up and take him to the café for dinner.

Thank You, Lord. Asher blew out a relieved breath. After thanking her and promising to send an update as soon as possible, he put his phone away and tried to focus on assisting the stranded seal. It wasn't easy. His thoughts wandered to Cameron and Tess far more often than they should. Mentally, he weighed the pros and cons of telling them both the truth. He still wasn't convinced that any good would come from it. Cameron was so young. Too young to understand the complicated circumstances that influenced his parents' and grandparents' decisions. And far too young to comprehend why Tess hadn't wanted to be a part of his life.

"He's rescuing a seal?" Eliana paused, her pen hovering over her notepad. "That's amazing."

Tess shot her sister a pointed look. There was no need for Asher to gain any more points in the hero category.

"I hope he takes lots of pictures." Cameron swiveled in a circle on the stool beside her. "Can I go and visit the seal sometime, Miss Test?"

"I'm not sure, pal." Tess couldn't bring herself to correct his mispronunciation. Or request that he call her Miss Madden. "That's up to the people who work at the sea life center."

"Maybe my dad can get us in." Cameron stopped spinning long enough to glance at the laminated menu on the counter in front of him. "Can we order now?"

"Absolutely." Eliana smiled. "What would you like?"

"A cheeseburger without the cheese, just ketchup, French fries and a chocolate shake." He tacked on an adorable smile. "Please."

"Whoa." Tess held up her palm. "Let's make that a vanilla shake, all right? Too much chocolate before bed is not a good idea."

If Asher didn't show up soon and she had to supervise Cameron's bedtime routine, it would go more smoothly if the kid wasn't amped up on chocolate.

"Aw, man." Cameron frowned. "No fair."

Eliana bit her lip, probably to keep from laughing.

"Staying up too late and being grumpy at school tomorrow isn't fair to Mrs. Franklin," Tess said. "You can still have what you asked for, but you'll need to have vanilla instead of chocolate."

He heaved a sigh. "Oh-kayyy."

This kid. Now it was her turn to smother a laugh.

Eliana wrote Cameron's order down. "And for you, my dear sister?"

"I'll have a chicken sandwich, please. No fries."

"Are you having a milkshake?" Cameron asked. "Because you'd better pick vanilla."

"Nope, not tonight." Tess tucked their menus back into the metal holder beside the napkin dispenser. "I'd like water, please."

"Coming right up." Eliana ripped the paper from her notepad, then turned and clipped it to the carousel in the service window separating the dining area from the kitchen. "I'll be back with your drinks in a few minutes."

"Thank you." Tess watched her sister move on to the next customers, a young couple who'd claimed stools at the opposite end of the counter, and marveled at Eliana's ease with helping people feel welcome in her café.

"What's my dad going to eat?" Cam's brow furrowed. "He'll be starving."

How sweet. Such a thoughtful boy. Tess turned her stool and faced him. "He'll probably grab something on his way home."

"Why can't we order him a dinner here?"

Tess glanced toward the service window. The cook had already plucked their order from the carousel. In the background, burgers sizzled on the grill, filling the air with a mouthwatering aroma. "I'll ask Eliana to add a sandwich and chips to our order. How does that sound?"

"Who's Eliana?"

"The lady who just took our order. Fun fact—she's also my sister."

Cameron sucked in a breath, his mouth forming a perfect O. "No way."

Tess chuckled. "It's true. Just like all the fun facts I share with you. We also have two other sisters."

His little shoulders sagged and he grew still. "I wish I had a sister. Or a brother."

The disappointment in his voice knifed at her. "I completely understand. Sisters and brothers are amazing. Maybe someday you will."

Oh, dear. That last part had slipped out before she'd given it careful thought. Asher's future, especially anything involving more children, was a hot topic she tried her best to avoid. She shouldn't have dangled that carrot in front of Cameron.

"I don't think so." Cameron shook his head. "My dad says it's just going to be us."

There it was, the perfect opportunity for her to ask about his mother.

"Well, well, what do we have here?" An older woman wearing an oversize parka the color of eggplant descended, bringing an oppressive cloud of heavy floral

Get ready to relax and indulge with your FREE BOOKS and more!

Claim up to FOUR NEW BOOKS & TWO MYSTERY GIFTS – absolutely FREE!

Dear Reader,

We both know life can be difficult at times. That's why it's important to treat yourself so you can relax and recharge once in a while.

And I'd like to help you do this by sending you this amazing offer of up to FOUR brand new full length FREE BOOKS that WE pay for.

This is everything I have ready to send to you right now:

Try **Love Inspired® Romance Larger-Print** books and fall in love with inspirational romances that take you on an uplifting journey of faith, forgiveness and hope.

Try **Love Inspired® Suspense Larger-Print** books where courage and optimism unite in stories of faith and love in the face of danger.

Or **TRY BOTH!**

All we ask in return is that you answer 4 simple questions on the attached Treat Yourself survey. You'll get **Two Free Books** and **Two Mystery Gifts** from each series you try, *altogether worth over $20*! Who could pass up a deal like that?

Sincerely,

Pam Powers

Harlequin Reader Service

Treat Yourself to Free Books and Free Gifts.

Answer 4 fun questions and get rewarded.

We love to connect with our readers! Please tell us a little about you...

	YES	NO
1. I LOVE reading a good book.		
2. I indulge and "treat" myself often.		
3. I love getting FREE things.		
4. Reading is one of my favorite activities.		

TREAT YOURSELF • Pick your 2 Free Books...

Yes! Please send me my Free Books from each series I select and Free Mystery Gifts. I understand that I am under no obligation to buy anything, as explained on the back of this card.

Which do you prefer?

❏ **Love Inspired® Romance Larger-Print** 122/322 IDL GRDP
❏ **Love Inspired® Suspense Larger-Print** 107/307 IDL GRDP
❏ **Try Both** 122/322 & 107/307 IDL GRED

FIRST NAME   LAST NAME

ADDRESS

APT.#   CITY

STATE/PROV.   ZIP/POSTAL CODE

EMAIL ❏ Please check this box if you would like to receive newsletters and promotional emails from Harlequin Enterprises ULC and its affiliates. You can unsubscribe anytime.

LI/SLI-520-TY22

HARLEQUIN Reader Service —Here's how it works:

perfume with her. Tess stifled a groan when she recognized the mayor's wife. Her piercing gaze made Tess's scalp prickle as she claimed the empty stool on the other side of Cameron. Oh, she shouldn't have let Cam talk her into sitting at the counter. A booth would've been so much better. This woman was far too curious.

"Hello." Tess offered a terse smile. "Can we help you?"

"Mrs. Lovell, are you behaving yourself?" Eliana appeared on the other side of the counter and set a shake garnished with whipped cream and an orange-and-white-striped straw in front of Cameron. The warning glance Eliana fired her way was easy to recognize.

Ah. Mrs. Lovell made everyone nervous. Good to know. Tess had overheard grumbling in the teacher's lounge about her meddling in a recent fundraiser.

"Of course, dear." Mrs. Lovell's smile didn't quite reach her eyes and her too-red lipstick was smudged on her front teeth. "I just wanted to get a good look at this handsome boy."

Ew. Tess resisted the urge to slip a possessive arm around Cameron's shoulders.

Cameron clutched his frosty glass with both hands and took a long sip.

"He's Sharon Hale's grandson, right?" Mrs. Lovell's dark eyes found Tess's.

Tess nodded.

"Is she talking about my grammie?" Cameron whispered, a mustache of whipped cream adorning his mouth.

Tess nodded and tried to offer an encouraging smile. *I've got you.*

"He reminds me of someone." Mrs. Lovell's eyebrows scrunched together. "I can't quite put my finger on it."

"He looks like his dad." Eliana impatiently clicked the end of her pen. "Can I get you anything?"

Ignoring the question, Mrs. Lovell tapped her red lacquered nails on the Formica countertop. "Where is your daddy tonight, young man?"

None of your business. Tess opened her mouth to offer a benign answer, but Cameron beat her to it.

"He's rescuing a seal." Cameron's sneakers thunked against his stool's pedestal as he took another sip of his shake.

"Is that so?" Something undecipherable flickered in the woman's expression. "How interesting that he'd leave you with these ladies."

"We always look out for each other around here, you know that." Eliana straightened the salt and pepper shakers, bottled hot sauce and container of sweetener packets on the counter. "Are you sure you don't want anything? Maybe a slice of pie to go?"

"No thanks." She slid off the stool. A smile that could only be described as victorious formed on her lips. "I got what I came for."

"Have a good night." Eliana nibbled on her thumbnail and watched her go. When the bells on the door jangled, indicating the woman had left, Tess shivered.

"Why did she come here if she didn't want to eat?" Cameron asked.

"Good question, buddy." Eliana frowned. "She's probably fishing for information."

Cameron giggled. "You can't fish for information, you silly head."

Tess's phone chimed with an incoming text. She

glanced at the screen, expecting an update from Asher. Instead, a message from Ben floated in a blue bubble.

I hope you don't mind that I asked Rylee for your number. Or that I'm making a bold move here... Frankly, I can't stop thinking about you and I'd like to continue that conversation we started on the dock. Are you free next Friday for dinner?

Wow, okay. Warmth heated her skin and she felt a smile tug at her mouth. Got to admire a guy who had the courage to send that text. And she was most definitely available. Without hesitating, she sent a text back and accepted his invitation.

Still smiling, she put her phone away and met Eliana's curious gaze. "Good news?"

Tess shot a pointed look toward Cameron. She didn't want to talk about Ben in front of him. *I'll tell you later*, she mouthed silently.

Eliana's brow furrowed.

"Order up." The cook slid two plates of food onto the counter, saving them from any further discussion.

Eliana turned and retrieved their food, then set their meals in front of them. "Enjoy."

"Thanks." Tess helped Cameron pour ketchup into the space between his fries and his burger, and tried not to think about his desire for a sibling. Or his revelation that Asher said they'd always be a family of two. That bothered her more than it should. Because it shouldn't matter. She'd given up her right to care about Asher and his future happiness when she'd broken his heart and turned her back on their baby.

Chapter Seven

Snow fell in wet flakes, making Asher's windshield wipers work double time. His headlights bounced off the spruce tree in the front yard as he steered his truck into the driveway.

Home. Finally. He shifted into Park, then turned off the engine.

Slouching against the seat cushions, he blew out a long breath. He hadn't felt happy to be here since they'd moved in. Most of the time he battled a fierce mixture of doubt, regret and guilt he couldn't quite shake.

But tonight, the golden glow emanating from the living room window meant he wasn't coming home to a lonely house with packed boxes stacked in the garage. Tess was inside. She'd responded to his desperate text for help without complaining. Once again, she'd dropped everything to care for Cameron.

And he was the biggest dirtbag in the world for keeping the truth from her.

Leaning forward, he rested his forehead against the steering wheel. *Lord, I'm in too deep. This has spun so far out of control. Please help me make it right.*

Exhausted, he trudged toward the door, hunching his shoulders against the snow falling inside his collar.

Before he could put his key in the lock, the dead bolt clicked and the door swung open. Tess waited on the other side, already slipping on her jacket.

"Hey." She offered a quick greeting, then shoved her feet into her boots. "How's the seal?"

Asher stepped inside and closed the door. "The seal's recovering, safe and sound at the rescue center. How's Cameron?"

"He seems fine. Went to bed about an hour ago. I haven't heard a peep. Hope you don't mind that we had some popcorn and watched an episode of *The Great British Baking Show.* I made sure he brushed and flossed his teeth, and I read him a story."

So Cameron had invited her into their evening ritual. That was a big deal.

"Not a problem." Hesitating, he unzipped his jacket. This was the first time he'd been alone with her. No distractions. No audience. The perfect opportunity to tell her about Cameron. "Do you need to go?"

"It's getting late. I have to be at school by seven thirty tomorrow morning."

"Right." He pulled off his knit hat and raked his fingers through his hair. "We haven't talked—really talked—since Cameron and I moved back."

Her brows tented. "I don't have much to say. If this is about Cameron and his reading, I can give you an update after his next session."

"Do you ever think about us, Tess?"

Her beautiful eyes widened. His heart jackhammered in his chest. *Please, please say yes.*

"Why are you asking?"

"Because I need to know." He stepped closer. Only inches remained between them. She didn't step back. "I need to know if you found what you wanted when you left."

"Does it matter?"

"It matters to me." A loose strand of hair had slipped from her ponytail. He reached out and gently tucked it behind her ear. The silky texture against his fingertips brought back memories. Memories that fueled his determination to ask these hard questions. "Do you ever wonder what might've happened if you'd stayed? If we'd married like we'd planned?"

"We would've been kids, struggling to raise a baby and go to school." Her words were barely above a whisper. "One of us probably would've dropped out of college."

"But we would've been together." He searched her face, longing for confirmation that being back home reminded her of their past.

She rubbed her fingertips against the hollow space above her collarbone. "It wouldn't have been enough."

"How do you know?"

Her gaze dipped to his lips. So she had thought about how good they were together. Emboldened by her subtle tell, he moved closer. "You were everything I ever needed, Tess. I would have worked three jobs, shoveled snow, bagged groceries, taken classes online—whatever it took—so we could be a family."

Her eyes found his again. Uncertainty lingered there. "Asher—"

He tipped her chin up with one finger.

Her lips parted. For one fantastic second, he clung

to the raw hope that he'd cracked the lock on her heart. He lowered his head and closed his eyes.

Her ponytail swished against the nylon fabric of her jacket as she shook her head and stepped around him. "I can't do this."

Asher dropped his chin to his chest and blew out a long breath. Rejected. Again.

Keys jangled behind him and the sweet fragrance of her perfume hung in the air. He didn't want to turn around. Should've known she'd blow him off.

"There's something I have to tell you. Cameron talked to me about having a sibling."

What? No. Panic shot through him. He whirled around. "When?"

"While we were eating at the café." She bit her lip, her hand on the doorknob. "I told him Eliana was my sister and that's when he said he wished he had a sister or a brother."

"What did you say?"

"That maybe he would someday. Your personal life is none of my business, so I tried to choose my words carefully."

"Thanks for letting me know." He wiped his hand across his face, hating that his poor choices had landed them all in this nightmare. The courage that had motivated him to take a vulnerable step toward her had vanished on the heels of her rejection.

"You're welcome." She opened the door and stepped out onto the porch, then turned back. "Asher, I—"

"Thank you for helping us out. Good night, Tess."

He closed the door and rested his forehead against the wood. *Hale, you're an idiot.* Why did he believe he could rekindle a relationship with her? Add it to his growing list of epic failures. And now that Cam had said he wanted a sibling, it wouldn't be long before he'd start asking more questions about his mother.

Your personal life is none of my business...

Groaning, he bumped his forehead against the door three times. She was his person. There had never been another woman for him besides Tess. Had he ruined any hope of a future together?

With trembling fingers, Tess unlocked the door to her place and hurried inside.

The TV lit up the dark living room. Worse, her sisters were lined up on the couch watching *Hope Floats*. Not only the best movie of all time, but also the one guaranteed to turn her into a pathetic puddle of tears.

And she did not want to cry.

Sidestepping a near kiss had almost done her in. She swallowed back a groan and quietly shut the door.

"How'd it go?" Eliana popped up off the couch and walked toward her, holding a green-and-white-striped bowl full of popcorn.

Someone else muted the volume, setting off a chain reaction of more questions.

"Did you have fun?"

"Did Asher thank you profusely?"

Her mind served up an image of Asher dipping his head to kiss her. She covered her face with her palm. Poor decision. Her silence gave away her predicament.

"Uh-oh." Eliana moved closer. "What happened?"

"Nothing," Tess murmured into her hand. She did not want to debrief with her sisters. Not tonight. Maybe not ever. All she wanted was to devour a pint of the butter pecan ice cream she'd hidden in the freezer and read the romantic suspense novel she'd borrowed from the library. With only two chapters to go, she'd find out if the hero rescued the heroine from her kidnapper and savor the details of their happily-ever-after. Because she'd butchered her own opportunity at a future with Asher and Cameron.

"Sure looks like something." Eliana's warm fingers gently clasped her wrist and tugged. "Want to talk about it?"

Tess dropped her purse and car keys on the floor. "I was ready to leave as soon as Asher came home, but then he brought up the past and we almost kissed."

Mia gasped.

"Told you." Rylee hopped up from the couch and did a ridiculous dance. "You owe me a latte, El."

Tess glared at her sisters. "What's that supposed to mean?"

"I said you and Asher would kiss tonight, and Eliana said you wouldn't." Rylee's smile faded when her eyes met Tess's. "Probably shouldn't have mentioned this. Sorry."

"We didn't kiss." Tess peeled off her jacket and hung it up, then pushed past Eliana and stomped into the kitchen. "You better not have eaten all the ice cream."

"They didn't actually kiss, so you'll have to buy your own latte," Eliana called over her shoulder and followed Tess into the kitchen. She set the popcorn bowl on the counter. "Don't worry. No one ate your butter pecan."

Rylee and Mia joined them. The stools scraped on the floor as they grabbed seats and circled around the kitchen island.

Tess rummaged in the drawer for the ice cream scoop. "Do you want to talk about it?" Mia plucked another kernel of popcorn out of the bowl. "Some of us are good listeners."

"Hey." Rylee elbowed her. "I'm a great listener."

"I told you. He brought up the past and asked me if I thought we would've survived if we'd kept our baby and raised him together." Tess pried the lid off the pint of ice cream. "I said it would've been a struggle, but he said that was fine because we would've been together, that he would do anything for me, blah, blah, blah."

"Oh, that is so sweet." Rylee clasped her hands under her chin. "He still loves you."

"Stop. It." Tess pointed the ice cream scoop at Rylee. "Love doesn't buy diapers or pay the rent."

"Wow, okay." Rylee held up her palms. "All I'm saying is that Asher still cares about you and that should count for something."

Sometimes Rylee made her want to scream. Tess pressed her lips together and dropped a generous serving of butter pecan into her bowl.

"Have you learned any information about Cameron's mother?" Mia crossed to the cabinet and pulled out a bowl. "Do you know where she is?"

"I've been tempted to look in Cameron's file at school, but I haven't."

Yet. Tess took a bite of her dessert and savored the sweet, creamy texture.

"Cameron is a wonderful boy. I'm sure his mother is so proud of him, wherever she is." Eliana leaned against the counter and watched as Mia reached for the ice cream container.

Tess grudgingly nodded. She didn't want to share but didn't need to eat the whole thing by herself.

"I don't think she's in his life," Rylee said. "Are there any pictures of her at the house?"

"No, but Cameron said some of his stuff is still packed in the garage." Tess lifted a shoulder. "I didn't see any photo albums lying around, either."

And she'd had plenty of opportunity to snoop after Cameron had gone to bed. There weren't any albums or framed pictures, except for a few of Asher and his siblings on the bookshelf in the living room.

"Maybe that's on purpose," Eliana said. "If they didn't part on good terms, Asher's probably not ready to have any pictures up."

"I'm surprised she let Asher move out of state with their kid." Mia added ice cream to her own bowl. "Most parents with joint custody can't do that."

"If she left them, she doesn't get joint custody, right?" Rylee asked, almost triumphantly.

Tess shot her another warning glance. Why did she have to sound so hopeful about a broken family?

"I noticed Asher doesn't wear a ring." Eliana tossed a kernel of popcorn in the air and caught it in her mouth.

"Wow, you all have done some research," Tess said.

"All I'm saying is this woman isn't fighting for her man." Rylee waggled her eyebrows. "You and Asher can pick up where you left off."

"No. We can't." Tess took the whipped cream Mia had brought from the fridge and added some to her bowl. "She had to have been his girlfriend while he was away at college, and I was only a brief distraction while he was home on break. Then he went right back to her apparently."

"Don't say that." Eliana rubbed her arm. "Asher loved you. Possibly still loves you."

"Oh, not you, too." Tess shot Eliana a disgusted look. "If he loved me, then why did he cheat on me and start a family with someone else?"

"Because you said you didn't want him," Mia said softly. "He thought your relationship was over."

"But he was *unfaithful*," Tess insisted. "I can do the math, Mia. He has children who are almost the same age with two different women."

Mia said nothing and took a bite of her ice cream.

Tess studied her. Why was she defending him?

"Don't you believe in second chances?" Rylee asked. "Think of this as a fresh start."

She shook her head. "I can't risk that kind of heartbreak again. Besides, it's awkward with Cameron involved. I—I can't hurt his feelings by dating his father, knowing it won't last."

"How do you know if you don't try?" Eliana asked. "Cameron obviously loves spending time with you."

Tess looked away. Cameron was a great kid. She enjoyed spending time with him, too. But he couldn't be the reason she gave a relationship with Asher another shot.

"I have a date with Ben on Friday. I've been telling myself I need to move on, and he is the perfect opportunity."

"Oh, brother." Rylee and Mia exchanged glances. "If you're trying to avoid heartbreak, then I'd stay far away from Ben."

"Why?"

"He's not into serious relationships," Mia said. "We'd hate to see you get hurt when you're so…fragile."

"I'm not *fragile*." Tess slammed her fist against the counter, earning more concerned glances. "A fun, casual night out with a handsome guy is exactly what I need."

Her sisters' expressions told her she couldn't be more wrong. Whatever. They clearly still had soft spots in their hearts for Asher. So she'd almost kissed him. Big deal. It didn't change their situation. She'd chosen a closed adoption for their baby, and he'd gone back to Oregon and the woman waiting in the wings. No matter how much she cared about Cameron, there was no way she'd let his dad break her heart again.

On Thursday afternoon, Asher forced himself to leave work on time to pick Cameron up from Tess's classroom. Not that the migratory patterns of puffins held his attention. He was still embarrassed about trying to kiss her. He'd spent the last twenty-four hours trying not to blush every time he thought about it. Evidently his efforts were failing, because he stood in the middle of her classroom, warmth creeping up his neck.

"Have you been to the library yet?" Tess handed him a piece of paper. "I made a list of books Cameron might enjoy reading with you, and I'm hosting story time this Saturday at eleven o'clock if you'd like to join us."

"Thanks." Asher took the paper from her, focusing on the glossy surface of her petal-pink nail polish and avoiding eye contact.

"Can we go to story time, Dad?" Cameron slid his folder inside his backpack, then zipped it closed. "Please?"

"I'm not sure." Asher folded the paper and tucked it inside his pocket. "We've got a busy day."

Tess huffed out a sigh. "Right."

That got his attention. He stared at her. "Is there a problem?"

"I find it hard to believe that you're too busy for a quick story." She crossed her arms over her chest. "Last time I looked at the schedule for the festival, your name wasn't on the volunteer roster. If I'm not mistaken, my sisters and I are covering for *your* mother."

"Thanks for the feedback." Anger swelled inside. She had no idea how difficult it was being a single parent with a full-time job and a mother with health issues.

"You're welcome." She turned around to help Cameron get ready to leave. "Don't forget your jacket."

"Thanks." Cameron snagged his jacket from the back of the blue plastic chair and shoved his arm into the sleeve. "Are you going to the carnival, Miss Test? My grammie has a booth and she said there will be real live fish."

"That's what I heard." Tess forced a smile. "Sounds exciting."

"Bye." Cameron slid his arm around her waist and squeezed.

Asher heard her sharp intake of breath. She glanced at Asher, panic flashing in her eyes. She gave Cam an awkward pat on the shoulder.

"Good job today." She disentangled from his hold. "Maybe I'll see you on Saturday."

"Yep. See ya." He snatched his backpack off the table, then trotted toward the door. "C'mon, Dad."

Asher lingered, his hands jammed in the pockets of his green cargo pants. Tess gathered her lunch bag, purse and car keys.

He stole a quick glance toward Cameron in the hall-way, staring at the artwork posted on the bulletin board outside Mrs. Franklin's room. He moved closer to Tess. "Tell me the truth," he said quietly. "Is this helping?"

"Reading together is always a good idea." She twisted her car keys in a circle around her finger. "He's such a tenderhearted child. Eager to please, too."

"Answer my question, please."

"Every week he recognizes a few more sight words and—"

"It's not enough, is it?"

She hesitated. "We can keep going."

"If he needs to see someone off the island for testing, I need to get that scheduled," he said.

"What are you guys talking about?" Cameron bounded back into the room, his face flushed. "Do I have to go to the doctor, Dad?"

The fear in Cameron's eyes made Asher's chest hurt. "You might have to see someone in a few weeks. We don't know yet."

Cameron's eyes welled with tears. "But I don't want to see a doctor. I hate needles. Please don't make me go. I promise I'll read more books with you."

"Oh, buddy." Asher held open his arms. "Come here."

Cameron burst into tears and flung himself at Asher. He swept his son into a hug and exchanged glances with Tess. The moisture in her eyes hinted at her own heartache.

Help. He silently pleaded while Cameron sobbed into Asher's jacket.

She cleared her throat. "I'll tell you what. How about if you guys keep reading together at home, come to story time if you can, and I'll ask Mrs. Franklin to set up a meeting next week."

Cameron pulled away and swiped his face with the back of his hand. "So no doctor?"

"We'll see." Asher smoothed his palm over Cameron's hair. "I'm proud of you, pal."

Cameron hung his head. "Can we go home now?"

"Yes." Asher kept his hand on Cameron's shoulder. "Thank you, Miss Madden."

She gave him an empathetic nod. "See you next time."

Asher followed Cameron out of the classroom. Uncertainty weighed every step. Out in the hallway, the custodian vacuumed the carpet. Cameron pushed through the double doors and Asher trailed him into the frosty evening air.

"How's a doctor going to help me read better?" Cameron kicked at a pebble in his path. "I don't want to go."

"I heard what you said." Asher fought to keep the fear from his voice. He had spoken to Krista for over an hour on the phone about Cameron's learning challenges. She had counseled him to follow Mrs. Franklin's advice and stay positive. No matter what. "Everyone learns differently. Sometimes we need a doctor to help us understand exactly how you learn."

"Why can't Aunt Krista help? She was my doctor for always."

"You're right." Asher pulled his keys from his pocket as they walked toward the truck. "She lives in Oregon and we live here now. Someone in Alaska who helps kids with these types of…things is better."

"I don't wanna go." Cameron climbed into the truck and slammed the door.

Me, either. He climbed in and slid behind the wheel. "Why don't we stop by and see Grammie?"

"Okay." Cameron shoved his backpack down by his feet, then buckled his seat belt. "If she has cookies, can I have one?"

Asher couldn't help but smile. "Maybe."

"Can I have two cookies?"

"Now you're pushing your limits, aren't you?"

"Pushing my limit?" Cameron wrinkled his nose. "What's that mean?"

Asher's stomach twisted. Cam looked so much like Tess when he made that face. The resemblance was unmistakable.

Lord, what have I done?

How had she not seen it yet? Maybe because she didn't want to.

Chapter Eight

This was not the Hank's that Tess remembered. Hearts Bay's oldest restaurant had completely renovated its 1970s-era dining room. Gone was the scuffed linoleum, rickety tables and chairs with torn upholstery. She scanned the rustic space with its exposed beams overhead and new round tables adorned with white tablecloths. Candles flickered in black lanterns-turned-centerpieces. The aroma of something delicious wafted toward her.

"What do you think?" Ben stood beside her, grinning. His sandy-blond hair was still damp in places, although he wore it in a slicked-back Brad Pitt kind of way that totally worked for him.

"This is amazing." Tess clutched her handbag and returned his smile. Oh, how she wanted this night to be amazing. Needed it to be amazing. Because she had to prove to herself that almost kissing Asher meant nothing. It was past time to move on. Time to stop living with one foot in her childhood memories and one foot itching to step forward into the future.

"It has a great vibe." His green eyes roamed the room. "I haven't lived here long enough to have seen the original restaurant, but I've heard the transformation is impressive."

"You have no idea."

"May I help you?" A young woman with Hank's dark eyes and ebony hair glided toward the podium in front of them. She had to be Hank's daughter, Gina. The little girl had been a preschooler once upon a time, and Tess and her sisters took turns babysitting Gina and her brother.

"A table for two, please." Ben put his hand on the small of Tess's back and she didn't pull away. The warmth of his hand felt…nice. No sparks, though. Yet. Well, the night was young. Besides, this was only their first date.

Gina plucked two menus from the rack behind her. "Follow me."

Ben gestured for Tess to go first. She followed Gina across the dining room to a cozy table for two with a lovely view of the far end of the island. The sun spilled its last rays across the mountains on the other side of the bay. Boats in the harbor bobbed in the water. Ben pulled out her chair for her.

"Thank you." She sat down, noting the unfamiliar fragrance of his aftershave. Spicier than she preferred. Not outdoorsy and fresh like Asher's.

She gave that pesky observation a mental shove and smiled at Ben. "You clean up nice."

Oh, brother. Not flirty and fun at all. More like cheesy and trying-too-hard.

He'd traded his plaid shirt and faded jeans for a crisp white button-down, olive green slacks and the kind of dress shoes you rarely saw a guy from Alaska wearing out to dinner. Ben met her gaze and winked as he took the seat opposite hers.

"You look beautiful tonight." One side of his mouth curved up, revealing a dimple she hadn't noticed before.

"Thanks."

She ducked her chin and smoothed the cloth napkin across her lap. No need to confess that she'd changed her clothes four times before Eliana approved her black dress and animal-print heels. A little fancy for dinner out on the island but she didn't care. This evening represented a mile marker on her journey. So she didn't feel the spark of attraction. That didn't mean he wasn't worth dressing up for.

"How long have you lived in Hearts Bay?" She picked up the menu Gina had left on the table.

"It'll be a year next week." He leaned back as a young man stopped at their table and delivered two glasses of ice water. "Rylee said you moved back to teach school?"

"I was born here and lived here until..." She stumbled at this part of her story. In college and during graduate school, she'd always managed to skate over it. Deflected the questions and asked about the other person. But Ben had asked Rylee about her. How much had her sister shared? Surely not everything.

"Tess?" He prompted her to continue. "Are you okay?"

"I'm fine." She straightened the flatware on the table-cloth. "I lived here until I went to college and graduate school in Fairbanks, then stayed to teach school. I'm not sure if Rylee mentioned we lost our brother, Charlie, in a fishing accident. That made me realize I wanted to come back home and be close to family again." Throat thickening with the words, she reached for her water and took a long sip.

Empathy filled Ben's kind eyes. "I've heard about Charlie. I'm sorry for your loss."

Setting her water down, she tried to stay present, but through the window behind him, she spotted Mrs. Hale, Asher and Cameron walking toward the restaurant.

Oh no. No, no, no. Not here. Not now.

"Do—do you have family nearby?" She stumbled over her words and resisted the urge to guzzle the rest of her water.

"My family is in Minnesota. They didn't quite understand my desire to move up here, but they visit as often as they can and they're happy for me." He shifted in his chair to follow her gaze, then turned back. "Are you sure you're all right?"

"Why?"

He searched her face. "You're a little jumpy is all."

"I'm sorry." She scooted her chair closer to the table and rested her chin on her clasped hands. There. He had her full attention. "First dates make me nervous."

His gaze held hers. "Me, too."

Really? He didn't appear uncomfortable at all. "What are you going to order?"

Before he answered, Cameron darted across the restaurant and slammed into her legs. "Hey!"

She steadied her water glass. "Hey, Cameron."

His brow crimped as he glanced at Ben. "Who are you?"

"Hey, little man." Ben held out his fist. "My name's Ben. What's your name?"

"Cameron James Hale."

When Cameron left him hanging without bumping fists, Ben's smile faded. "It's nice to meet you."

"Why are you here with *him*?"

"Cameron." Heat flamed her cheeks. She scrunched her napkin in her fists. This was getting worse by the second.

Asher and Mrs. Hale caught up to Cameron. "I'm sorry he interrupted." Asher's gaze bounced between Tess and Ben, his mouth twisting.

Tess averted her eyes. The whole restaurant probably saw her heart fluttering in her throat. Super awkward.

"Ben, this is Cameron's father, Asher Hale, and Cameron's grandmother—"

"Sharon Hale." She thrust her uninjured arm out. "It's a pleasure to meet you, Ben."

He shook her hand. "Likewise."

"Let's go." Asher clamped his hand on Cameron's shoulder and tried to guide him away.

"But I want to sit with her," Cameron whined.

"We're not interrupting Tess's date." Asher leaned down and whispered something in Cameron's ear. He nodded, his chin wobbling, then he slunk away without looking back.

"Enjoy your evening." Asher gave them an apologetic look, then followed Cameron and his mother toward a table on the opposite side of the dining room.

Ben's confused expression sent an uneasy sensation skating down her spine.

"I didn't realize you had a kid."

"What?" Her hands trembled. "No, he's a student at my school and I tutor him."

Ben's doubtful gaze pinged across the room and back. "Really."

"You don't sound convinced."

"Because he—never mind." A muscle in his jaw flexed. "It's none of my business."

She stared at him in disbelief. Seriously? He'd let a brief interruption ruin their evening?

Ben reached over and covered her hand with his own. "I'm sorry." He huffed out a nervous laugh. "I didn't mean to upset you. It's just the dad—Asher—gave me that look like he'd caught me with his girl."

"We're not together. I mean, we were, but that was a long time ago."

"I see."

She tugged her hand free from his and retrieved her menu. "I'm ready to order. How about you?"

Her stomach churned like it did when she'd flown in Rylee's plane. Ben's comments squelched the anticipation she'd carried with her into the restaurant. She couldn't eat. Not now. Because everywhere she went in Hearts Bay, she collided with Asher and Cameron. Encounters that forced her to confront a past she'd tried to forget. How could she possibly move on when regret nipped at her heels with every step?

"Why is she with that guy?" Cameron grudgingly obeyed Asher's instructions to leave Tess alone, but he walked across the restaurant as though his sneakers weighed a thousand pounds. "Why can't we sit with her?"

Asher glanced at his mother over Cameron's head. She'd clamped her palm over her mouth to keep from laughing. Super. So she wasn't going to be any help, either. He should've known Mom would find humor in this debacle. Taking a lighthearted approach was just one more way for her to deflect, to pretend she hadn't played a part in this tangled web.

The hostess led them to a table toward the back of the restaurant. His mother chose the seat that allowed her not to see Tess and Ben's table. How convenient. Asher didn't protest, though. Surely he could sit in a restaurant while his ex-girlfriend had dinner with another guy. Maybe they were just friends. He shouldn't assume it was a date. Except the look the guy shot him when Tess made the awkward introductions hinted at his intentions.

"Is there a kids' menu?" Cameron sat on his knees in the wooden chair, craning his neck to see the options on the table.

"Absolutely." The hostess smiled and handed him a paper menu folded in a square and a pack of four crayons wrapped in plastic. "Your server will be right with you."

"Thank you." Asher slid into the chair beside Cameron, then helped him take off his coat. "What would you like to eat?"

"What do they have?"

Asher bit back a sharp comment about looking at the menu. If Cam couldn't read it, then that wasn't helpful. Or kind. He helped him unfold the menu and spread it on the table. Thankfully, there were pictures, words and plenty of blank space to draw a picture. Word searches and unscrambling letters on these things were always a nightmare to navigate.

"Chicken fingers and fries. No dippy. Just ketchup." The plastic crinkled as he unwrapped the crayons. "May I have chocolate milk, please?"

"No chocolate." Asher ruffled his hair. "Too close to bedtime."

"But it's Grammie's birthday." Cameron offered his best puppy-dog stare. "Please?"

"Nice try. The answer is still no. Especially if you plan to order dessert. We have to go easy on the sugar, pal."

Cameron heaved a sigh. "Oh-kaaayy."

Asher ignored Cameron's hangdog expression and studied the menu instead. "Wow, Hank has really stepped up his game. Have you tried the baked halibut, Mom?"

"It's one of my favorites." Mom surveyed the restaurant. "He's always busy."

Asher pretended to look around, but he let his gaze return to Tess. Well, the back of her, anyway. That was enough, though. Ben leaned in and said something, then grinned. She laughed and the familiar sound made its way across the room and threaded around Asher's banged-up heart. She didn't want him. Didn't want to be a mother. She'd been clear about her plans and dreams for the future and had no intention of including him. Nothing about her preferences had changed.

She had every right to see other people. So why did he care so much whom she spent time with?

"Miss Test has a nice laugh," Cameron said. "I wish she'd come sit with us. She likes to color, just like me."

Asher sucked in a breath. He dragged his gaze back to meet his mother's. This time she didn't laugh. Regret flashed in her eyes, then vanished. She shifted in her chair and offered a bright smile.

"Let's play a game," Mom suggested. "We each share a highlight from our day."

"A highlight?" Cameron stopped coloring and stared at her. "What's that?"

"It's something good that happened to you today," she said. "I'll go first."

Of course. Asher slung his arm across the back of Cameron's chair. This wasn't exactly a game. More like an opportunity for her to talk about herself. But if it kept them all distracted from the other guests in the restaurant, then he'd play along.

"I booked two new vacations for some of my favorite clients." She held up her casted arm. "Not bad for a lady with one arm."

"I won two tetherball games at recess," Cameron said.

"Good for you." Mom glanced at Asher. "What's your highlight?"

Not going out of my mind with jealousy when I see Tess out with someone else. He scrubbed his fingertips along his jaw. "The seal we rescued is doing much better."

"Can I go to the bathroom?" Cameron dropped his crayon on the table and hopped off his chair. "I gotta go bad."

"Sure." Asher turned and pointed toward the doorway behind them. "It's right through there. Do you need me to go with you?"

"Nope."

As soon as Cameron was out of sight, his mother leaned across the table. "You should tell him the truth."

"What?" Asher shook his head. "No way. He's too young. He wouldn't understand."

"But he adores Tess. Everyone can see that. He'll be thrilled that she's his—"

"I can't." Asher held up his hand. "Not yet."

"Why not?"

"Because I'm not ready." The words came out with more force than he would've liked. "Tess didn't want to be a mom."

Her eyebrows sailed toward her spiky hair as she flipped over her menu and scanned the back. "They're both going to find out eventually. It's only going to get harder the longer you wait."

"Why the sudden change of heart, Mom? You've seemed quite content to go along with this charade. It's a big island and all that. Isn't that what you said when we first got here? What's going on?"

She lowered the menu. Her eyes swam with pain. "I'm worried that if you wait too much longer the truth will come out in a way that will make reconciliation impossible."

"Mom, she's right over there, having dinner with someone else. If your grand plan is to get us back together, I don't think that's a valid reason to confess what we've done."

"You need to tell the truth because it's the right thing to do." She shot a glance toward the server approaching their table. "And my grandson needs to know his mother."

Well, she'd picked a fine time to suddenly follow her moral compass. He clamped his mouth shut, determined not to ruin her birthday with an argument, but she was wrong. He couldn't tell Tess that Cameron was her son. It would wreck the fragile bond they'd established. Worse, Cameron would flip out. He was only seven years old. And no matter how much he wanted freedom from the secret that held him prisoner, he couldn't fathom turning his little boy's entire world upside down.

The little boy reminds me so much of your brother, Charlie... Didn't realize you had a kid... Asher gave me a look...

"You're being ridiculous," Tess growled as she paced from the fireplace to the kitchen, where an empty carton of butter pecan sat beside the sink. Mrs. Franklin's comment about Cameron reminding her of Charlie and Ben's reaction to seeing Cameron and Asher at dinner tonight spun through her head on repeat.

She leaned against the counter. The ice cream she'd devoured a few minutes ago made her stomach hurt. Sure, she could chalk the comments up to coincidence. Mrs. Franklin had taught a lot of brown-haired, brown-eyed boys in her career. It probably wasn't unusual that some mischievous students reminded her of Charlie when he was a second-grader.

But Ben's assumption that Cameron was her son had filled her with an uneasy feeling she couldn't ignore. Was she Cameron's mother? That hardly seemed possible. The baby she'd given birth to had been adopted. How could Asher have thwarted those plans and kept Cameron from being placed with the family she'd chosen?

Everyone in town had heard that Asher met someone and married her right after he'd left. Maybe on the rebound and that's why it hadn't worked out?

Either way it didn't matter.

And her inability to think about anything else had ruined her dinner date. Ironic, since she'd silently fumed at Ben for letting Cameron's interruption spoil their fun.

They'd declined dessert at Hank's and Ben drove her home. After a chaste kiss on the cheek at her door, he'd stated he didn't want to get in the middle of whatever was going on with her and Cameron's dad.

As much as his parting words stung, she couldn't blame him. Clearly, she wasn't ready to start a new relationship, not with the way she was obsessing over Asher and Cameron now. To be honest, the more time she spent with them, the more she regretted the harsh words she'd flung at Asher all those years ago. As it turned out, she desperately wanted to be a mom.

And what was she supposed to do now? Call Asher and say "Hey, remember that baby I had? Well, I made a horrible mistake"?

Instead, she reached for her phone to summon her sisters for an emergency meeting, then changed her mind. They were hanging out at Mia's. She had a text waiting in their group chat with an invitation for her to join them. She hesitated, checking the time on the oven's digital clock. Only nine fifteen. Not too late to sit around the fire on a Friday night. If no one else was there, maybe she'd even share her thoughts with them. Except her sisters would have questions. Questions she couldn't answer. Not to mention, they'd only fuel her wild speculation. No, she needed to keep this to herself for now.

She tucked her phone in her purse, put on her jacket and her boots, then grabbed her keys and hurried out the door. Outside, a stiff wind stung her cheeks. Snow crunched under her boots as she walked toward her car. Inside, she shivered as she started the engine. After adjusting the defroster, she shifted into Reverse, then drove to Mia's place. A half dozen cars lined the road on either side of the one-level rambler Mia inherited after Charlie had passed away.

Refusing to let memories of her brother discourage her from joining the gathering, Tess parked and circled around the side of the house. In the backyard, a crowd of at least twenty people made her steps falter. So maybe she wouldn't be baring her soul to her sisters tonight.

"There you are." Eliana waved and motioned for Tess to join her beside the fire. "Pull up a chair."

Flames licked the edges of the pallets, sending sparks into the indigo sky. The night air carried a crisp, tangy bite, hinting that more snow was on the way. Tess shivered, wound her scarf tighter over her jacket, then dragged an empty canvas chair closer to the firepit.

"This is nice. I'm glad Mia invited people over to hang out," Tess said.

"Yeah, I'm glad she did, too." Eliana stood. "I'm going to get some food. Want anything?"

"In a minute." Tess rubbed her hands together. "I ate too much ice cream."

"Uh-oh." Eliana hovered over her. "Everything okay?"

Tess waved her off. "Go grab something to eat. We'll catch up later."

Eliana patted Tess's shoulder, then walked away. Tess leaned forward and held her palms out, determined to soak up some of the warmth. Too bad she'd forgotten her gloves. Mia would probably loan her a pair, but then she'd have to go inside. Friends trickled toward the firepit, carrying small plates of food and insulated mugs. They dragged chairs over and formed a ring around the fire. Snippets of conversation and laughter filled the air. She hated to give up her seat just to go find gloves.

"Is there room for one more?"

A tingle shot down her spine at the familiar sound of Asher's voice.

She smiled at him, then scooted her chair over. "Sure."

"Thanks." Asher arranged his blue canvas chair beside hers, then sat down. "Did you want coffee or hot cocoa?"

"I'm good, thanks."

He nodded, then took a sip from his silver insulated mug. Studying his profile, she was rocketed back in time to another party, where they'd snuggled beside a fire in a friend's backyard. Promised each other that nothing would ever change. That they'd be together for always.

The memory pinched at a place deep inside. Asher had made her so happy back then. Part of her wondered if they could start over. He caught her staring. The fire cast shadows across his face, making it hard for her to read his expression. She felt the warmth of his gaze and shifted in her chair.

"What are you thinking about?"

You. Us. "That humans love to sit around fires together."

Okay, so that wasn't exactly what she was thinking. But if she told him the truth, that he'd nudged open the door of her heart all over again, what would he say?

"We've had some good times around a fire, haven't we?"

Ah. He'd taken a trip or three down memory lane, too. She scampered back to safer territory. "Where's Cameron?"

"He fell asleep on my mom's couch." Asher wedged

his mug between his knees. "I'll crash in her guest room tonight so I'm there when he wakes up."

"Good plan."

Asher glanced at her. "Where's Brent?"

"Who?"

"Brent. The guy you were having dinner with."

His inquiry sent her thoughts into another tailspin. Especially since his tone carried a bit of an edge. Was he asking to make conversation? Or did he want to know if she and Ben were dating? "His name is Ben, and we're just friends."

"Oh."

She bit her lip to keep from asking how he felt about that piece of information. He took another sip of his drink. Maybe to hide the smile playing at the corners of his mouth?

"Are you glad you came home?"

Shivering, she blew on her hands.

"Here." Asher clasped his fingers around hers, then tucked their hands inside his down vest. The warmth of his touch combined with the soft fabric of his sweater against her skin made her breath hitch. He hadn't held her hand in years, yet somehow it was like no time had passed at all.

"W-what was the question?"

He chuckled. The familiar sound twined around her heart and suddenly she didn't want him to ever let go. It would be so easy to forget about their complicated history. To forget the heartbreak. What if she told him that she'd made a horrible mistake?

"I asked if you're glad you moved home."

Oh, she really didn't know how to answer that. Staring into the fire, she measured her words carefully. "It's good to be with my sisters and parents again. I'm loving my job."

"You sound a little uncertain." The pad of his thumb caressed the back of her hand. "Island living has its perks."

She couldn't look away. Her mouth felt dry. His lingering stare sent them skidding right back into the danger zone. And wow, the warmth of his touch muddied her thoughts. From the corner of her eye, she saw Mia and Rylee huddled on the other side of the firepit, launching curious glances her way. Mia's expression silently warned, *What do you think you're doing?* Tess estimated she had less than thirty seconds to move away from Asher before one of her sisters interrupted.

This wasn't a good time to dig up the past.

"I'd better go." She pulled her hand from Asher's and stood. "Busy day tomorrow."

"I'll walk out with you." He left his mug and chair and followed her across Mia's backyard.

Her heart hammered as she retraced her steps around the side of the house. They were alone. Sort of. This could be her opportunity to ask him about Cameron's mother. To demand the truth so she could squash these frantic thoughts rambling in her mind once and for all.

She stopped beside her car and faced him. The words died on her lips. With one look at those gorgeous eyes of his, all her intentions faded. He reached past her and grabbed the door handle but didn't open it. The familiar scent of his aftershave wafted toward her. Yet another memory surfaced, reminding her of lingering goodnight kisses. Those tender moments when they couldn't get enough of each other.

His gaze slid to her lips. Her heart took flight, soaring like an eagle over the ocean. She shouldn't kiss him. Really, she shouldn't. That would complicate their already messy relationship.

But she didn't care. The aroma of smoke from the fire filling the air, the stars and a sliver of moon in the night sky and her hand still tingling from the warmth of his touch conspired against her. She clutched the lapels of his down vest with both hands, then pressed up on her toes and brushed her lips against his.

He gently cupped her face with his palms in a gesture so tender her knees went wobbly. Oh, how she'd missed this. Missed him. He tasted sweet, with hints of chocolate from the cocoa he'd been drinking. When he deepened the kiss, she responded, sliding her hands along the down fabric of his vest until her fingers met at the nape of his neck. She tipped her chin up, releasing a delicious sigh as he kissed the tender skin along her jaw.

Suddenly he released his hold and pulled from her grasp. The cool air smacked her and she had to stifle a whimper.

"What? What's wrong?"

Chest heaving, he wiped his face with his palm. "We can't do this."

"Why not?"

"Because. It's…not right. I'm sorry, Tess."

Wait. That's it? "I—I don't understand."

"You should go."

The silvery-blue light from the streetlamp cast a shadow over half his face. Still, she didn't miss the tormented expression twisting his features. She averted her gaze and fumbled for her keys in her purse, then quickly slid behind the wheel. She wanted him to call her name. To stop her from leaving.

But he didn't. To make matters worse, he closed her door for her. A firm dismissal.

"You're *sorry*?" Choking back a sob, she started the engine. She was the one who was sorry. Oh, she'd been an idiot. She should've demanded more information, and instead she'd thrown herself at him. *So* humiliating. Thankfully, their meeting with Mrs. Franklin was scheduled for Tuesday. They'd have to discuss Cameron's inability to read. And it would break her heart to stop tutoring him, but she had to step away. It was better for everyone involved if Asher found someone more qualified to help.

Chapter Nine

Man, he'd messed up.

Asher's back protested as he pushed to a seated position on the futon in his mother's guest room. The hurt in Tess's eyes was seared in his memory. She'd surprised him when she reached up and pulled his face toward hers. Not that he was complaining. At all. He'd kissed her back.

Until his conscience prodded him to tap the brakes. Too bad his words came out all wrong. Kissing wasn't the problem. It was the deception. And now he'd made the whole situation ten times worse by letting their relationship get complicated.

Again.

Straightening to his full height, he grimaced and rubbed at the ache in his neck. What he wouldn't give for another hour of sleep followed by a hot shower.

"Daddy?" Cameron's muffled voice filtered in from the hallway. "Where are you?"

"Right here, pal." Asher crossed the room in three quick strides and opened the door. "Good morning."

Cameron stood barefoot, wearing the same jeans and

T-shirt he'd worn to dinner the night before. He rubbed his fists over his eyes. "Why are we here?"

"You fell asleep on Grammie's couch last night after we came back from dinner. I didn't want to wake you so we had a sleepover."

"My clothes are too scratchy. I wish I had my jammies." He yawned. "I'm hungry. Can we have waffles?"

Asher tamped down a groan. Mornings that started with complaining usually spiraled into tears and a meltdown. "Let's see what Grammie wants to eat. Waffles have a lot of sugar. That might not be the best choice."

Cameron growled and stomped his foot. "You're always talking about sugar. Stop it!"

"Cameron James Hale." Asher knelt in front of him. "That is not how we speak to one another. Do you understand me? We can't feed Grammie a breakfast that's loaded with sugar because it might make her sick."

"But waffles don't make me sick. They make my tummy happy," he whispered, his lower lip trembling and eyes glistening with unshed tears. "Please, Daddy."

Maybe it was the slab of concrete futon he'd slept on or the pathetic look in his son's eyes that made him give in. "All right, waffles it is. Only if you have some scrambled eggs first, though."

Cameron sniffed and dragged his arm across his nose. "Can I help stir?"

"Sure." Asher reached out and pulled him into a hug. "I love you, buddy."

"Love you, too, Daddy." Cameron flung his arms around Asher's neck and leaned into him, melting away any remnants of irritation. What he wouldn't do to protect this tenderhearted little guy.

"Come on, let's go see if Grammie's awake." Cameron pulled away and raced toward the kitchen. "I want to tell her I slept on her couch all night."

Asher chuckled, then pushed to his feet. He saw a stack of mail on top of the bookshelf beside the door. Hesitating, he studied the return address. Looked like a bill from the utility company. He rifled through the other envelopes stacked underneath. Two credit card bills, plus a bill from the local hospital and another from the radiologist.

His scalp prickled. Was Mom struggling to pay her bills? If he asked, would she give him an honest answer?

Trailing after Cameron, he found his mother sitting at the kitchen table in her bathrobe.

"Good morning, boys." She swirled her spoon through the bowl in front of her. "Sleep well?"

"I slept all night on your couch, Grammie." Cameron bunny hopped around the table. "In my clothes. So weird, right?"

Her smile didn't quite reach her eyes. "I saw you sleeping there. We tried our best not to wake you."

"Dad says we can make waffles." Cameron found the plastic step stool in the pantry and dragged it toward the stove.

A tendril of steam curled up from her mug. "Waffles sound delicious."

"I'll fix eggs and bacon, too," Asher added. He'd offset all those carbs with protein. "Do you have any?"

"There's plenty of both in the fridge. I'm going to be good and stick with my oatmeal, though."

Well, that was progress. He didn't want to scold her about her blood sugar, especially not first thing this morning. "How's your arm feeling?"

She shrugged her shoulder. "It hurts."

Asher turned to find Cameron pulling the egg carton and a half gallon of milk from the fridge. "Whoa, bud. Let me help you."

"Okay, but I want to crack the eggs."

That sounded like a disaster. "How about you help stir the oil into the waffle mix instead?"

"But how will I learn if you never let me try?"

Mom chuckled. "Good question."

Asher shot her a look. Not helping.

"Cam, if we're going to do this we need to work together. And you're going to have to listen."

Cameron quirked his mouth to one side, then nodded. "Deal."

Wow, these two are full of surprises this morning. "Great. Why don't you find a mixing bowl and a measuring cup."

Asher crossed to the pantry, grabbed a glass bottle of maple syrup and the cooking oil, and brought them to the counter.

"What do you two have planned for today?" Mom asked. "Anything fun?"

"Story time at the library." Cameron plunked a glass mixing bowl onto the counter. "Grammie, where are the measuring cups?"

"In the drawer next to the silverware," she said.

"We're also going to get your groceries and fix your garbage disposal." Asher went to the fridge to get the bacon. "Is there anything you need at the hardware store? I didn't see a shovel in the garage. Do you have anyone lined up to shovel your driveway? We're expecting a storm."

Her silence gave him pause. When he nudged the refrigerator shut with his shoulder, then turned around, she fixed him with an icy glare. "You don't need to do all that. I'm not helpless. I know how to hire someone to shovel snow."

"You don't have to call anyone. That's what I'm here for. To help."

Why was she refusing to let him?

Her gaze swung toward Cameron. He'd climbed onto the stool and had ripped open the box of waffle mix before Asher could stop him.

"Hang on a sec—"

Too late. Waffle mix spilled all over the counter, completely missing the measuring cup.

"Oops." Cameron grimaced. "Sorry, Daddy."

Asher blew out a long breath. "It's okay. Let's try again. Maybe use a spoon this time?"

"Okay," Cameron whispered, hanging his head.

"I'm sure you have plenty to do without spending your Saturday running my errands." Mom lifted her mug to her lips and blew on her coffee. "Did I hear that Tess Madden's in charge of story time now?"

Message delivered. She wanted him to talk to Tess. As in tell her everything. Except after last night's kiss, he wasn't quite sure how he was going to pull that off seeing as how she probably wasn't speaking to him.

"I noticed a stack of bills in the guest room." He dampened a paper towel and wiped up the spilled mix. "Anything you want to talk about?"

Mom's eyes narrowed. "You're reading my mail now?"

"I didn't read anything," Asher said. "They're sitting right there on the bookshelf under the light switch."

She pressed her lips into a thin line.

"Mom, if there's anything you need, please ask."

"You know what I need? I need you to stop trying to fix everything." She stood, wobbled, then shoved back her chair. "I didn't ask for your help."

Her voice broke and she turned, stumbling over a remote-control car that Cameron had been playing with the night before. Asher held his breath. Thankfully, she regained her balance and hurried from the room.

Cameron burst into tears. "You hurt Grammie's feelings," he wailed.

Oh, brother. Asher dropped his chin to his chest. He'd made Tess cry and now his mother and son, too. Why was this happening?

Rejected twice in one night. That had to be a new personal low.

Tess slid her purse under the table that doubled as her workspace in the children's corner of Hearts Bay's community library. The pain of last night blanketed her like a thick fog. Drawing in a deep breath, she tried to focus on the familiar aroma of books mingling with Mrs. Fairweather's floral perfume.

"Okay, dear. Here you are." Mrs. Fairweather's bracelets jangled as she set a disposable cup of coffee with a plastic lid on the table beside a stack of children's books. "Anything else I can get you?"

Tess forced a smile. "I'm all set. Thank you."

"You're welcome. It's a privilege to have you here today. The children will love you."

Hot tears stung the backs of her eyes and Tess reached for the coffee, grateful she had a distraction. Reading to kids normally brought her such joy, but today she could hardly keep her emotions in check. Throughout her childhood, she'd lived for Saturday morning story time at the library. Mrs. Fairweather had the uncanny ability to make the characters in the books she read aloud seem so real. With her cheerful smile and chestnut hair twisted into a long braid, she hadn't changed a bit.

"Have fun." Her dark eyes held an unspoken question as she gave Tess a careful once-over, but she didn't say anything else. When she returned to the desk toward the front of the library, Tess blew out a long breath.

The fact that it was her turn to sit in her favorite corner of the library and share a story out loud should have put a bounce in her step. Another person in the community she'd admired for years now regarded her as an equal. It was an honor that Mrs. Fairweather had invited Tess to take over story time. Her eight-year-old self would've turned cartwheels across the gray carpet.

Instead, she wiped her sweaty palms on her jeans for the second time and let her eyes wander toward the clock on the wall. It was almost eleven, which meant any minute now, children would walk through the double doors and claim their spots on the floor at her feet. A collection of stuffed animals and hand puppets sat against the wall, under a beautiful mural that depicted familiar scenery from the island. The upper level of the library featured more books and a small meeting area. A couple of diligent teenagers sat at a table, their computers open in front of them. The vaulted ceiling overhead offered plenty of room for a gorgeous mobile featuring lifelike renditions of bald eagles and other birds of prey commonly found on Orca Island.

This had been her happy place for so long. Why was she such a nervous wreck?

Through the windows facing the parking lot, she saw

Asher and Cameron getting out of Asher's truck. Her stomach coiled in a tight knot. Oh, why had she invited them? She'd hoped that after last night's embarrassing kiss, Asher would've kept Cameron away from the library this morning.

She wasn't ready to see them. Not yet. How in the world would she pretend everything was completely fine?

The automatic doors parted with a whoosh. Tess pasted on a smile and claimed her seat. Parents and children trickled in, their exuberant chatter filling the cozy library. Mrs. Fairweather greeted each warmly and directed them toward Tess, pausing to receive a handmade drawing from a first-grade girl Tess recognized from school.

Distracted by the sweet interaction between the little girl and Hearts Bay's beloved librarian, she lost track of Asher and Cameron.

"Miss Test!" Cameron's enthusiastic voice drew a chuckle from several onlookers. He darted toward her, grinning and leaving a trail of melted snow behind as he closed the distance between them.

"Cam, slow down," Asher called.

She quickly set her coffee down, then opened her arms. Hugging him was probably a dangerous move, but she couldn't possibly tell him no. Exchanging glances with Asher, she caught the alarm flashing in his eyes right before Cameron hopped into her lap.

"Whoa." She planted her feet firmly on the floor to keep from toppling off the chair, then gently clasped his shoulders with her hands. "Good morning, Cameron. How are you?"

There. Calm. Friendly. As long as she didn't look

at Asher again, she'd be fine. She felt her chin wobble and quickly bit her lip, willing her pulse to stop racing.

"I'm good." Cameron tapped the toes of his boots together, sprinkling more drops of water on the carpet. "We had waffles for breakfast. Bacon, too."

He did smell vaguely of maple syrup. She resisted the urge to reach up and tame a random strand of dark hair sticking up on the back of his head.

"Hey." Cameron's eyes roamed her face. "Why are your eyes all watery? You sick or something?"

She blinked quickly, then plastered an even bigger smile in place. "Nope, not sick." She lowered her voice to a whisper. "This is my first story time, so I'm a little nervous."

Cameron's eyes widened and he sucked in a breath. "Don't worry, you'll be great." Then he gave her arm a squeeze and hopped off her lap.

What a sweet child. His tender words settled around her like the throw blanket on her couch at home. Against her better judgment, she let her gaze travel to Asher. His brow furrowed as he leaned against the library's back wall.

Great. He was sticking around to listen. With both Asher and Cameron in the audience, how was she supposed to concentrate?

"Which book are you reading to us?" The little girl who'd offered her artwork to Mrs. Fairweather sat down on the floor beside Cameron. Aria, that was her name. Wasn't it?

"Aria, right?" Tess reached for the books she'd asked Mrs. Fairweather to pull from the shelves.

The girl nodded.

"Great question." She held up two books. The clear

plastic jackets crinkled in her hands. "Would you like to start with *The Day the Crayons Quit* or *Llama, Llama Mess, Mess, Mess*?"

"Crayons!" Aria bounced up and down. "That's my favorite."

"Llamas!" Cameron punched the air with his fist. "Animals rule."

More children joined them, calling out their preferences as they claimed spaces on the carpet.

Tess couldn't help but laugh. "I'll start with crayons, then the llama story and finish up with *Room on the Broom*."

Before they could share more opinions, she opened the book and started reading. Her voice quavered at first and anxiety zipped through her veins, but slowly, sentence by sentence, she gained confidence.

She could do this. One story at a time. Then a few questions, some small talk, and she'd be out in less than an hour.

Then she'd figure out how to survive tonight's fall festival. Surely Asher and Cameron would be there. And she was helping at a booth they shared with Mrs. Hale. Somehow she'd have to pretend that nothing had changed. Because even though she'd savored that kiss, Asher had made his feelings quite clear when he'd pushed her away. There wasn't space in his life for her anymore. Which meant she'd have to get used to not spending time with Cameron, either. The very thought gutted her. Mrs. Franklin was going to be so disappointed when she realized Tess had failed at teaching Cameron to read.

Asher leaned against the library's back wall, his eyes riveted on Tess. Man, she was good at this. The dozen kids fanned out in a semicircle at her feet gave her their undivided attention. Sure, they wiggled and squirmed. A few were lying on their tummies, tapping their toes against the carpet, with their chins propped on their little hands.

But they weren't whispering or poking each other. Impressive.

Asher stole a glance at the handful of parents hovering nearby. Most stared at their phones. A lady standing beside him swayed back and forth, wearing an infant in a front carrier.

As Tess opened another book and brought the characters to life with her animated voice, laughter rippled through her small audience. She smiled and turned the page. Oh, that smile. Despite his best effort last night to end that incredible kiss, putting space between them was like trying to douse a house fire with a bucket of water. He couldn't help himself. He was as captivated as the little kids attending story time.

He glanced toward Cameron sitting in the front row. Asher half expected him to lose interest and ask to leave, but he sat staring up at Tess, hugging his knees to his chest. From this angle the similarities between Cameron's profile and Tess were hard to miss. His stomach dropped like a rock plunging into the sea.

Had anyone else noticed? His mother's warnings filtered through his head again. She was right. Frankly, he hated to admit that, but he was asking for trouble, trying to keep Cameron's identity concealed. Folks in this town weren't shy about sharing anything. As soon as someone figured out the connection between Cameron and Tess, word would spread like the stomach flu. He pushed his fingers through his hair, torn between breaking free from the lies and protecting Cameron from getting hurt.

Tess finished the third story, closed the book, then smiled at the kids. "Who has questions? Raise your hand and I'll call on you."

She set the stack of books at her feet as the kids stretched their arms toward the ceiling and begged her to call on them. "Me. Pick me" echoed through the children, wiggling like salmon in a feeding frenzy.

Tess pointed to a little girl in an orange dress printed with yellow and brown leaves. She wore matching orange leggings and sat quietly, her hand in the air. "Yes, Aria. What's your question?"

"Do you have a favorite children's book?"

Asher smiled. He already knew the answer. Tess had read her copy of *The Boxcar Children* until the pages fell out and the cover was worn away. When they were younger, he'd take it and hide it just to get her attention. Then she'd get so mad that she wouldn't speak to him until she found her beloved book or he caved to her demands and gave it back.

They'd made so many incredible memories together over the years. She'd been his best friend. His confidante. When their friendship morphed into something more as teenagers, he'd fallen head over heels in love. Yes, they had made a poor choice that night when he'd visited her while he was home from college on break. They'd gone too far. And getting pregnant had devastated Tess.

But since he became a believer, he'd learned that their past mistakes didn't condemn them forever. They could walk in freedom now. Cameron had a father and a mother, living in the same town. Standing here watching her lead story time with their son at her feet, hanging on her every word, Asher realized that he still loved her. More than anything, he wanted all of them to be out from under the burden of guilt and shame.

She had every right to be angry with him. It might take a long time for her to move past the deception once she learned the truth, but he clung to the hope that maybe, just maybe, they could move forward. Together.

Tess dismissed the children and Asher moved to retrieve Cameron before he got distracted.

"Excuse me, please." He scooted past two moms talking over their strollers parked side by side. "Cameron, come on, buddy."

Cameron's face fell. He glanced back at Tess. "But—"

"We've got to get going." Asher angled his head toward the door. "You'll see Miss Madden later."

"Dad." Cameron frowned. "I want Miss Test to come with us."

Asher glanced at Tess. Was she listening? He couldn't tell. Although Cameron's voice was hard to miss in such a small space. She collected the books, her purse and a coffee cup, then turned toward them. When her eyes met his she tried for a smile, but she couldn't hide the hurt. Or the purple spots under her eyes. Poor thing. She looked as stressed out as he felt.

"What do we have to do next?" Cameron grabbed Asher's hand and tugged on it.

"We have to go to the store and get groceries for us and for Grammie. And I promised her I'd try to fix her garbage disposal because it's broken."

"That's boring stuff. Miss Test, do you want to go to the café for lunch with us? We can see your sister."

"Cameron, we're not going to the café for lunch," Asher said. "I just told you we have to help Grammie."

"But we always have to help Grammie," Cameron moaned. "I want to have lunch with Miss Test."

"Thanks for the offer but I'm going to have to say no this time." Tess shifted her books to her other arm. "Tonight's the fall festival and I have some things I need to do first."

"Oh, yeah, the festival." Cameron's expression immediately brightened. "Are we going?"

"We have to get all of our errands and our chores done, which is why we'd better get going." He held out his hand toward Tess. "Can I carry anything for you?"

She shook her head. "No thanks. I'll return these to Mrs. Fairweather on the way out."

Asher nodded. An awkward silence blanketed them. "See you later."

"Yep. See you." She brushed past them and walked toward the front desk. Asher and Cameron trailed behind. This was so weird. Pretending like nothing had changed was harder than keeping a secret.

He watched her hand the books to the librarian, then she slung her purse strap over her shoulder and walked outside. Just like last night. And like last night, he wanted to go after her, pull her into a hug and tell her that they were going to figure this out. Somehow. But he didn't have the right to offer her a gentle reassurance that this was all going to work out for the best, because he was the one who'd created this debacle. He didn't have the luxury of offering her those hope-filled words because he'd crushed her last night. And when she found out she was Cameron's mother, how would he ever prove himself trustworthy again?

Chapter Ten

Eliana was right. They should've skipped the festival this year. Tess rubbed her temple, where a headache throbbed, then plastered on a smile and awarded a new goldfish to a delighted little girl dressed in a pumpkin outfit.

"There you go, sweet pea. Enjoy." Rylee waved. "Thanks for coming by."

Tess gave her sister a thumbs-up. What would she have done without Rylee's infectious enthusiasm? After the painful encounter with Asher outside Mia's house last night, followed by their interaction at the library this morning, hurt and confusion had dogged her all day.

"Step right up." Rylee cupped her hands around her mouth to form a megaphone. "The Maddens and the Hales invite you to Fish for Fun."

While Rylee welcomed more customers to their fishing game, Tess surveyed the crowded high school gym. Volunteers had collapsed the bleachers and transformed the floor into a sea of carnival games. Laughter, conversation and the occasional squeal of a happy kid echoed off the walls. The familiar aroma of caramel apples and popcorn made Tess's stomach growl. She'd stayed busy after story time, running errands and working out to avoid human interaction until the festival started. Then she'd chugged a smoothie and eaten a protein bar on the drive over to the high school.

She needed to tell her sisters that she'd kissed Asher. And soon. Because now more than ever, she craved their support. But part of her couldn't bring herself to admit that she'd misread the whole situation. He'd held her hand. Walked her to her car. What was she supposed to—

"Tess?" Rylee's voice tugged her back to the present. "Can you help our friends here get their fish, please?"

"Of course." Tess carefully filled two clear plastic bags with water and goldfish, then handed them to their new owners. "There you go. Enjoy."

The boys' eyes widened as they accepted their prizes. "So cool!"

After the boys and their parents moved on, Tess and Rylee had a lull in the line at their booth. She tried to stay busy mopping up water she'd spilled with a hand towel and using bleach wipes to clean the handles on the plastic fishing poles. Anything to keep moving and keep her mind occupied. She sensed Rylee's gaze on her as she brought the clean poles back to the table.

"Everything okay?" Rylee asked.

"Uh-huh." Tess scanned the crowded gym for any sign of Asher or Cameron.

"You seem distracted."

Tess shrugged and scraped her thumbnail at a stain on the table. Oh, she was terrible at hiding things, especially from Rylee. "Tired, I guess. People are serious about their fall carnival fun."

"Eliana and Mia will be here soon to take over." Rylee pulled her phone from the back pocket of her jeans. "She texted me a few minutes ago and said they'd be here by eight fifteen, so any minute now."

"Good. I'm ready for a break and something to eat."

"How was story time this morning?" Rylee retrieved her water bottle that she'd stashed underneath the table. "Anybody interesting show up?"

"Why do you ask?"

Rylee paused, then unscrewed the cap. "It's just a question."

"About twelve kids, mostly students from my school. The parents stayed and listened. Asher and Cameron came, too." She tacked that last detail on quickly, as if it didn't matter that they'd attended. "It was fun."

She pushed up on tiptoe and craned her neck when she thought she spotted Cameron's familiar red hoodie two booths down from theirs. So much for her grand plans to avoid Asher.

"You're looking for him, aren't you?" Rylee teased.

Tess met her sister's inquisitive stare. "Looking for who?"

She was terrible at stalling, too.

"Don't even try to pretend with me." Rylee put her water bottle back down. "You're looking for Asher. Or Cameron. Maybe both."

Warmth climbed her neck. "Maybe."

"If you want to go hang out with him I could probably handle this by myself. It's not—"

Tess shook her head. "I'm not leaving you here by yourself."

Or inviting myself to hang out with someone who doesn't want me. She bit her lip to keep from blurting out the painful truth.

"All right." Rylee gestured for a pack of tween girls lingering nearby to join them. "Step right up, ladies. It's time to fish for fun."

The girls exchanged nervous looks, then inched closer. They were a little old for this game targeted at younger children, but Mrs. Hale had ordered way too many goldfish, and Tess did not want to take them home. Or adopt them as her class pets.

Nearby a little boy let out an exuberant "Yes!" and Tess immediately whirled in the direction of the familiar voice. Cameron. He stood less than ten feet away, high-fiving Asher. Tess felt her mouth spread into a wide smile.

"Girl, you've got it bad," Rylee murmured.

She wasn't wrong.

Ever since story time, she couldn't stop thinking about what it would be like to spend a Saturday running errands or puttering around the house. Too bad Asher had squashed that daydream when he'd abruptly ended their kiss. Still, as she watched him ruffle Cameron's hair, a longing she couldn't ignore settled deep inside.

Pull yourself together.

She turned away and pretended to check on their goldfish. Rekindling her romance with Asher was a ridiculous idea. She had no business thinking about a future as Asher's wife and Cameron's stepmother.

"Miss Test has fish." Cameron yanked on Asher's shirtsleeve and pointed to the booth. "Can I have one?"

Gross. He'd rather shovel three feet of snow every

day for the rest of his life than own a goldfish. "How about we try the ring toss? Maybe you'll win another stuffed animal." Asher braced his hand on Cameron's back and tried to steer him away from the Maddens' booth. Far, far away.

Cameron stayed rooted in place, as if his sneakers were glued to the gym floor. "But this is Miss Test's and Miss Rylee's game. And Grammie helped with the booth, too. Why can't I play?"

Asher glanced at the fishing booth again and caught Tess watching them from her post behind the table. Her expression made him pause. If he wasn't mistaken, she looked almost happy to see him. But that didn't make sense. Not after the way he'd treated her last night. He had to speak to her. He had to explain. Everything. Even if that meant standing in line to win a goldfish he didn't want.

"All right." He let Cameron tug him toward the booth.

While they waited, Cameron kept his eyes glued on Rylee. She entertained each child and offered encouraging words as she handed over the plastic fishing pole. Tess and Rylee had hung a shower curtain dotted with pink, purple and teal sea creatures on a clothesline suspended between two posts. When a child cast the line over the shower curtain, the magnet in the fishing pole caught the plastic fish out of the portable swimming pool hidden out of sight. For the younger customers, Tess disappeared behind the curtain. Asher smiled at her kindness. Probably assisting to make sure every child caught a fish. Genius. That way none of the Maddens had to care for the leftover goldfish. They went home with all the kids waiting in the line.

Every time Tess reappeared, Cameron laughed with delight.

A rivulet of unease shot from Asher's spine to his toes. He felt like a monster. Cam was besotted with Tess. It wasn't right, keeping a boy from knowing his mother.

"Dad, can you hold my new stuffy, please?" Cameron thrust the stuffed orca whale he'd just won into Asher's arms. Asher opened his mouth to protest, then decided against it. He'd end up carrying the thing at some point, anyway.

The family in front of them collected their goldfish prizes, then stepped out of the way.

"Hey, guys." Tess smiled. "Are you here to fish?"

"Yep." Cameron did a goofy little happy dance that made Tess laugh.

This kid. Asher shook his head.

Mia and Eliana arrived at the booth. They exchanged hellos, then Asher and Cameron waited patiently while Rylee quickly explained how the game worked.

"Have you ever been fishing before, Cameron?" Tess handed him a blue plastic fishing pole. Asher winced. That was a detail a mother would probably know about her son, if she'd been a part of his life.

Tess's smile was a little forced. Her voice a little higher than normal. He was proud of her for trying to pretend everything was fine, but her fingers trembled as she tucked a loose strand of hair behind her ear. This was hard for her, too.

"I fished once with my uncle, Justin," Cameron said. "We didn't catch anything."

He held the pole with both hands and examined it. "Is this thing plastic?"

Tess nodded. "Your job is to cast it nice and easy over this bar here." She turned and tapped on the pole suspending the shower curtain. "There's a whole bunch of fish in that pool back there."

"Real ones? Let me see." Cameron ducked down and tried to peek under the table.

"No, no." Asher chuckled and gently tugged on Cameron's hoodie. "Don't peek. That's part of the fun."

"Okay, but I really want to catch a goldfish." Cameron straightened, his little brow puckered. "What if I catch two goldfish? Can we take them both home, Dad? And do goldfish get married?"

Tess's eyes widened. Rylee, Eliana and Mia burst out laughing.

Asher coughed, then cleared his throat. "So many questions, pal. Try and catch a fish first, okay?"

Cameron followed Tess's instructions and carefully cast his line over the bar and into the make-believe pond. Rylee ducked out of sight. Cameron's pole jiggled.

"Hey, I think I got something," Cameron squealed.

"Reel it in," Tess said.

Cameron pulled his pole up and a yellow plastic fish hung from his magnetic lure.

"Look at that." Tess clapped. "Great job."

Her smile faltered and she glanced at Asher. "I'm assuming it's okay if he gets a real fish?"

Asher blew out a long breath. "I don't suppose you'll let him live in your classroom?"

"Ha, nice try." Tess shook her head. "No class pets right now."

"Yay, a fish. I'm going to name him Nemo. Unless it's a girl, then I should name her Dory. Except she's not blue." Cameron tipped his head back and giggled, his dark eyes gleaming. His infectious laughter drew a look from Tess that Asher could only describe as pure joy.

Man, he couldn't stand keeping these two from each other. But what was he supposed to do? Just invite her into their lives? So maybe he wasn't the greatest single dad in the world but he was getting the hang of it. Selfishly, he wasn't ready to make any drastic changes.

A little boy needed his mother, though. And frankly, he'd been selfish long enough.

What would happen once he revealed that she was Cameron's mother? They'd need to talk about next steps. Probably should hire an attorney. A legitimate one. They'd need a co-parenting plan, too. Alaska had laws about this sort of thing. Since the adoption papers were fraudulent, she was likely entitled to 50/50 custody.

It all made his head spin, but it was time to accept responsibility for the choices he'd made.

"Miss Test, can you come with us? We still have more to see," Cameron asked.

Tess hesitated, avoiding Asher's gaze while she secured the top of the plastic bag with the goldfish inside.

"Go ahead," Mia and Eliana chimed in. "We got this."

Tess bit her lip and shot him a questioning glance, silently asking for permission.

"Sure, come on." Asher held out the stuffed orca. "I'll need your help carrying this."

"Fair enough." After tying her sweatshirt around her waist, she swung her purse strap across her body, scooted around the end of the table and joined them.

"Hand over the whale." Her fingers brushed his as she took the stuffed animal. A feeling of warmth zipped along his arm and he smiled. Her mouth lifted at the corners and their gazes locked. Parents and kids pushed passed them. Still they lingered, oblivious to the chaos swirling around the gym. He owed her an apology.

"Tess, about last night. I—"

"Cupcakes." Cameron yanked on Asher's arm again, jostling the goldfish and jarring Asher back to reality. At a table nearby, the cheerleaders were hosting a bake sale. A fundraiser for new uniforms, according to the poster taped to the table.

"How do we win those?" Cameron asked. "Is there a game?"

Asher frowned. Could he not read the sign? "You don't win them. The cupcakes are for sale."

"May I have one, please?"

"Sure, why not." Asher and Tess trailed Cameron toward the line forming at the cheerleaders' bake sale. They'd eaten beef stew and fresh fruit at his mother's house after he'd finished repairing the garbage disposal. Not exactly an award-winning meal, but he didn't feel quite so bad about letting him have a cupcake now.

Asher sneaked a glance at Tess. She fiddled with the strap on her purse, her expression pinched. Regret knifed at him. He hadn't apologized. Not the way he wanted to. She deserved more than an abbreviated conversation in a crowded gym.

Not to mention the whole truth about Cameron.

But what if he'd waited too long? That incredible kiss only made a messy situation more tangled. If he'd told her the truth already, would tonight be the first of many outings? Oh, he wanted to believe it was possible. He really did. But he couldn't forget her insistence that she'd never wanted to be a mother. Even though she was clearly an amazing teacher and kids loved her, spending time with other people's children was so much different from being a parent.

Had she changed her mind?

"Hi, Asher." Mrs. Franklin rolled a stroller beside him and parked at the end of the line. "Are you enjoying the carnival?"

He held up the plastic bag. "Proud owner of a new goldfish."

"Oh, what a treat."

"How about you?" He leaned down and peered at the sleeping baby snuggled inside the stroller. "Good-looking kiddo."

"Thank you. This is our new granddaughter. Too young to enjoy all this, but that didn't stop my husband and me from bringing her out." She glanced sideways at Cameron, chatting away with Tess as the line for the bake sale inched forward. "Looks like he's having a ball."

That's the problem. He stuffed down the inappropriate reply and managed a nod.

"I'm glad we ran into each other." She leaned closer. "Are we still on for our meeting after school on Tuesday?"

"Of course." He hoped the panic pumping through his veins wasn't evident by his expression. Silently, he willed Tess to keep Cameron occupied so he wouldn't hear their conversation. Asher had taken Cameron to see his new pediatrician. After Cameron passed the hearing test and Asher shared some of Tess's feedback, the doctor wrote a referral for further evaluation. Now they needed the recommendation from Mrs. Franklin. No matter how much Asher had tried to reassure Cameron that he wouldn't have to get any shots, the boy had still sobbed in the car on the way home.

Mrs. Franklin surveyed the crowd. "I've lost my husband. I'd better find him before we need to feed the baby. It's good seeing you, Asher. We'll talk more on Tuesday."

She unlocked the stroller's brakes, then maneuvered into the adults and kids milling around them. Her email said she wanted to talk about Cameron and next steps, but Asher knew what *next steps* meant.

Cameron couldn't read.

And no tutoring session with Tess, or library story time on Saturday mornings, or reading together every night from now until Easter would change that.

Tess caught his eye. "Everything okay?"

All he could manage was another pathetic nod. He wanted to tell her everything.

But he couldn't. Not now. He had to get Cameron through this visit off the island with a specialist first.

Man, it was going to be rough. Cameron was so fearful. It would be better if he waited. He couldn't introduce the trauma of Tess being his mother, too. That was all too much for his little boy to handle.

Besides, it wasn't like he was keeping Cameron's needs a secret from Tess. She knew all about his struggles with reading.

It wouldn't be easy, but he had to keep her maternity a secret. At least for now. As soon as they got back from seeing the specialist and he had a concrete diagnosis and a treatment plan, then he'd tell Cameron—and Tess—the whole sordid tale.

Chapter Eleven

She dreaded this meeting.

Tess crossed the hall to Mrs. Franklin's room, clutching her folder containing her notes about her sessions with Cameron. Six weeks had passed, and he'd shown little improvement. Worse, his latest assessment indicated he still wasn't reading at grade level.

She'd so hoped these tutoring sessions would help. Even though she suspected Cameron struggled with dyslexia, a part of her still wanted to impress Mrs. Franklin. The woman had been her hero for so long. Tess had wanted to prove she possessed the skills to make a difference. To show Mrs. Franklin and everyone else in the community she wasn't the same girl who'd made a mistake and gotten pregnant.

After Cameron's reaction last week when he'd overheard her conversation with Asher about a referral, she felt terrible knowing he'd have to go to an appointment that frightened him. Disappointment weighted her steps as she settled in the chair facing Mrs. Franklin's desk.

"Hello, dear." Mrs. Franklin glanced up from her laptop. "How was your day?"

Tess sighed and slumped against the chair's plastic back. "It was okay."

"Oh?"

"Asher will be so bummed when we tell him Cameron needs a referral."

Mrs. Franklin nodded. "It's always difficult to share this kind of news."

"Cameron is such a fun kid. I hate that he's struggling." She glanced around the empty classroom. "Where is he, by the way?"

"I sent him down to the library with Courtney. They're going to read together while we meet with Asher." Mrs. Franklin smiled. "We won't be long. This is just a formality."

Tess sat up straighter. "What do you mean?"

Mrs. Franklin reached for a can of sparkling water on her desk. "I'm fairly certain Asher knows we're recommending a referral, don't you?"

Snippets of their conversation followed by Cameron's outburst replayed in her mind. Tess tapped the end of her pen against her folder. "Probably."

Oh, why did this fluster her so much? Why couldn't she treat Cameron like any student who needed help? *Why* had she made helping him read her personal mission?

"I—I wanted to do more."

"You've done everything you could."

Mrs. Franklin's gentle encouragement did little to lift Tess's spirits. "But I let you down. Cameron, too. I want him to learn to read, and not just a little, but to catch up to his peers. That's not going to happen. At least not right away."

Wow, where did that come from? So embarrassing, pouring her heart out like this. Not to mention unprofessional.

Mrs. Franklin set her drink aside. "We can only do so much. There's nothing wrong with referring students off the island for more professional help."

Heat pressed against the backs of her eyes. She averted her gaze and fidgeted with the corner of the folder in her lap, her vision blurry. Stupid tears. *Why* was she getting emotional about this?

She shifted in her seat, then uncrossed and crossed her legs again. "I wanted this to go well." Her voice was barely above a whisper. "Every session, I thought maybe next time. Maybe next time something will click and he'll…"

"That's the joy and the struggle of teaching here in Hearts Bay. We're invested in our students' lives and their families are part of our community. We hurt for them, and that's a good thing."

Asher strode into the room, his keys jangling in his pocket. He barely made eye contact before claiming the seat beside hers. "Sorry to keep you waiting, ladies."

He shrugged out of his parka and draped it over the back of the chair. A shock of dark hair flopped over his forehead. Her pulse quickened and her eyes followed the path of his hand as he smoothed it back.

Mrs. Franklin cleared her throat and shot her a look. *Oh no.* Caught. The tips of her ears burned. Only thing worse than crying in front of Mrs. Franklin was her obvious reaction to Asher's presence.

"Thank you for coming in." Mrs. Franklin closed her laptop, then reached for a folder sitting on a stack nearby. "This won't take long. Cameron's in the library with one of our teaching assistants, so you don't need to worry."

Asher offered a curt nod. "Great. Thank you."

"Perhaps you're aware, Cameron continues to read below grade level." Mrs. Franklin slid her glasses into place and flipped the folder open. "Despite Tess's excellent tutoring for the last several weeks, Cameron's latest assessment reflects little improvement."

"What does this mean?" Asher scrubbed his fingertips along his stubbly jaw. "Are you saying he has a learning disability?"

Mrs. Franklin nodded. "You'll have to go off island for a thorough assessment, but there are several options available, either in Kenai or Anchorage."

He glanced at Tess. "Have you said anything more to Cameron?"

The defeat in his eyes made her stomach drop. "We're required to speak with you first."

"He's going to freak out." Asher hung his head. "Even though my sister is a pediatrician, he gets so upset about going to doctors' offices. We had our first visit with our new pediatrician. He's on board with the referral, but Cameron is terrified. This is going to be tough."

"If it were me, I'd choose the psychologist in Anchorage. She has a stellar reputation." Mrs. Franklin reached for her notepad and pen. "We'll give you the appropriate paperwork, of course, but here's her name and the practice's website. When you have a few minutes, read her profile. I think you'll be impressed."

Asher took the sticky note.

Oh, how she wanted to reach over and squeeze his arm. To offer support. She clutched her folder tighter.

"I—I can't find him."

"What do you mean?"

"I've looked all over the house. He's not here."

"I'm on my way." She ended the call.

Asher shoved his phone in his pocket, then took another lap through the house. He and Krista had covered the stranger danger topic with Cameron a half dozen ~~times~~. They even had a secret password established in ~~...~~ tried to convince Cameron to get in ~~...~~ But somehow he'd thought ~~...~~ worry about the

Not with Mrs. Franklin watching. Well, never, actually. *He doesn't want you anymore, remember?*

"If you don't mind, I'll call now. In case there are questions I can't answer, you both are here to fill in the blanks." Asher dug in his pocket, then pulled out his phone. "You're recommending Louisa Bridger?"

"Yes."

He punched the numbers into the keypad. Tess rubbed her clammy palms on her pants. What if the psychologist couldn't see Cameron until after the holidays? The poor kid would fall further and further behind. Her mind raced ahead to worst-case scenarios. A child who didn't receive proper intervention would get frustrated. Maybe even stop trying. Cameron already sensed he wasn't reading as well as the other kids. What if—

Stop. She mentally slammed the door on worrying. Mrs. Franklin was right. They could only do so much. Time to pass the proverbial baton to a psychologist.

A few minutes later, Asher ended the call. "Good news. They had a cancelation on Friday afternoon. If I can get tickets for the morning flight to Anchorage, Cameron can see her at two o'clock."

"That's wonderful." Mrs. Franklin clasped her hands under her chin. "What a blessing."

Asher stood and grabbed his jacket. "I'll pick Cameron up at the library on my way out."

Tess jumped to her feet. "We can walk out together."

The expression on Asher's face halted her steps.

"It would be better if I spoke to him alone." Asher brushed past her. "Thank you again for the referral, Mrs. Franklin. I'll keep you posted."

Tess clutched the back of the chair, staring after him

as he left the classroom. Wow, okay. Surely he didn't blame her for Cameron's challenges. Did he?

"Everything is going to be all right," Mrs. Franklin said. "You'll see."

"Right. Of course." Tess pressed on a smile, then returned her and Asher's chairs to the pod of tables beside Mrs. Franklin's desk. "Have a great night."

She hurried across the hall to her own classroom, anger bubbling up like a waterfall spilling over a cliff. So Asher wanted to handle this all on his own.

"It's fine," she whispered. "Totally fine."

Except Cameron was going to flip out and she'd only wanted to be there to help. To ease his fears. Why wouldn't Asher let her? He hadn't hesitated to call on her before. Grabbing her tote bag off the floor, she plunked it onto her desk, then shoved her laptop inside and added her water bottle to the side pocket.

She picked up her keys from the desk, strode toward the door and turned off the lights. If she'd clung to any hope at all that Asher wanted to be anything more than friends, his behavior just now had snuffed that out.

"Cam?" Asher sprinkled fish food into the goldfish's bowl Friday morning, then put the container back in the kitchen cabinet. "Cameron, it's time to go."

Cameron didn't make a sound. Why didn't he answer? Asher left the kitchen and checked the couch in the living room. Empty. An episode of *Paw Patrol* played on the television. He'd agreed to let Cameron watch a second episode while he finished cleaning up the breakfast dishes and packing their bags.

Stepping into the hall bathroom, he peeked behind the shower curtain. Empty.

"Cameron, this isn't funny. You need to come Now."

Asher left the bathroom and cut long strides to t end of the hall and Cameron's bedroom. His rumple navy blue-and-red-plaid comforter spilled over the side of the bed. A gray duffel bag sat on the floor. Cameron had dropped his pajamas on top, inside out. Yet another clue that he'd only halfway obeyed Asher's request t finish packing and get ready to leave fo. The red numbers on the beds 8:27. Their flight behind s

"C
o

Anchorage

...side table alarm clock said ...ook off at ten thirty. Great. Already ...chedule and they hadn't even left the house.

...ameron?" He turned and yanked the closet door ...en, praying he'd find his little boy crouched on the floor, stifling a giggle. Only a laundry hamper, a pile of stuffed animals and an empty suitcase greeted him.

Dread settled low in his gut. Cam hadn't taken the news of this trip well, and now he was nowhere to be found.

Whirling around, he pulled both pillows and the blankets off the bed. It was empty. Asher sank to his knees and looked under the bed. No Sammy the sea otter. And no Cameron.

Blood surged behind his ears. Where would Cam go? Was this about today's appointment or did someone take him?

Asher raced to the kitchen, his hands trembling as he fumbled for his phone. He scrolled until he landed on Tess's number and jabbed at the screen.

"Hello?"

"Is Cameron with you?"

"What? No, he's not. Aren't you leaving for Anchorage this morning?"

case someone ever ~~~~ a vehicle that wasn't safe. B~~~~ he had a few years before he had to w~~~~ kid sneaking out.

Rain pattered the windows in the living room. He'd checked the forecast before breakfast. Temperatures hovered around thirty-five degrees with freezing rain expected. If Cameron was outside, did he slip on his coat before he left?

Asher hurried out the front door without checking for any evidence of a jacket or hoodie left behind. There wasn't time. He shivered in the cold October air, squinting against the rain as he turned in a circle in the front yard. Where would a seven-year-old hide?

The shed. Asher took off in a frenzied sprint, racing around the side of the house toward his father's workshop. A gray structure shaped like a small barn sat in the backyard's corner. With shingles and a front door, it made an appealing hideout, but Cameron had only asked about it on the day they'd moved into Dad's house.

Still. He had to look. For his own peace of mind. "Cameron!"

No answer.

Chest heaving, Asher stopped in front of the shed and jiggled the doorknob. Locked. He cupped his hands around his eyes and peered in the tiny window beside the door. The glass was grimy, and he couldn't see much, other than a lawn mower and a bunch of tools.

His mind raced, terrifying scenarios flashing through his brain like a car chase in a bad-movie trailer. What if Cam had walked across a busy intersection and a car didn't see him? Or maybe he'd wandered down to the water's edge to throw rocks and slipped—

Stop. He shook off the horrific notion and spun away from the shed's door. A quick peek behind the structure revealed what he expected. No sign of Cameron.

Although he didn't want to tell her, keeping this news from Mom wasn't an option. Cameron might be on his way to her house. He had to let her know. Even though she'd freak out. Pulling out his phone while he cut long strides across the yard, he scrolled to her number.

The call went to voice mail. He left a message explaining that he couldn't find Cameron and they'd have to delay their trip to Anchorage. If he didn't find him soon, they'd miss their flight. Hopefully that was the worst-case scenario.

Please, Lord. Help me find my boy.

"Eliana, wake up." Tess rushed into the dark bedroom and pounced on her sister's lumpy form, burrowed under the floral duvet on her bed. "I need your help."

"Go away." Eliana yanked the duvet over her head. "Too early."

"Cameron's missing." Her voice broke. "We have to look for him."

"What?" Eliana flung the covers back and sat up. "How did you hear?"

Tess swallowed back the lump in her throat and

grabbed the discarded jeans and hoodie lying on the floor beside the bed. "Here. Put these on."

Eliana plucked her phone from the nightstand. "I'm texting Mia and Rylee first."

"Good idea." Tess dropped the clothes on the end of Eliana's bed and backtracked until she found her own phone where she'd left it on the kitchen counter. Asher had sent another text.

Search party meeting at the community center in 10 minutes. Will divide up in small groups.

My sisters and I will start at our parents' house first. Is that okay?

Asher texted back a thumbs-up emoji.

A few minutes later, they'd hopped into Tess's car. The rain fell sideways, an unforgiving mixture of nearly frozen precipitation.

"I can't imagine a child wandering alone in this weather," Eliana said, fiddling with the end of her braid. "Where could he have gone in such a short amount of time?"

Tess gripped the steering wheel tighter and leaned forward, struggling to see through the fog and the rain pounding her windshield. Eliana's question made her stomach queasy with dread.

"We have to find him." She'd keep repeating those same five words, as if Cameron would reappear because she willed a positive outcome.

Her phone hummed with an incoming text message. "Can you read that for me, please?" The defroster blasted on high, but condensation still fogged the glass, making it difficult to navigate the road leading to their parents' place.

Eliana plucked Tess's phone from the cup holder in the console. "It's from Asher. He says they've spoken with all the neighbors on his mom's street. No news yet. Another group will check The Tide Pool and the café because those are Cameron's favorite restaurants."

Tess's throat tightened. He was so little. Too young to be walking that far alone, especially in a storm. She slowed the vehicle as they rounded a curve in the road. What if he wandered into the woods and an animal chased him? Had Asher taught him how to handle dangerous encounters?

Eliana squeezed her arm. "We won't stop looking until we find him."

Tess nodded, then blinked back tears. If only she'd done a better job of helping Cameron process his fears. He must've run off because today's trip to Anchorage and his appointment scared him. She should've tried harder to intervene. Encouraged Asher to do more to ease his concerns. Maybe then they wouldn't be searching for him in the middle of a storm.

She shook away the shame and the guilt and focused on steering the car into her parents' driveway. Getting bogged down in her regrets wouldn't help. She couldn't change the past. A reality she was learning to embrace.

Mrs. Lovell was getting out of her car when Tess parked beside her father's truck.

"What is she doing here?" Eliana grumbled.

"Mom mentioned she wanted to sell her guest room furniture and buy something more suitable for the cottage, in case Grandmother moves in." Tess turned off the ignition. "Maybe Mrs. Lovell is here to check it out."

Eliana pulled her hat from her purse and put it on. "Instead of shopping for furniture, maybe she should help look for Cameron."

"Agreed." Tess jammed her phone into her coat pocket, then tugged on her hat and gloves and hopped out of the car. Rain pelted her cheeks like stinging needles. Her mother stood on the porch with Mrs. Lovell.

Tess offered a quick wave.

"I'll go in and hang with Mom for a minute," Eliana said. "Text me if you find him."

Tess gave her a thumbs-up, then hurried around the side of the house toward the guesthouse. She couldn't explain why she felt compelled to look there. Except that Cam had loved visiting her parents' house and had chattered on and on about all the tools her dad used to finish the flooring in the kitchen.

She opened the door and stepped inside. The smell of lumber and fresh paint greeted her.

"Cameron?" She closed the door quietly. "It's me. Miss Tess."

Silence.

"If you can hear me, please come out."

She scraped the moisture from her boots on the entryway floor mat, hesitating when she spotted a pair of familiar dirty sneakers on the floor nearby.

Thank You, Lord, for keeping this precious boy safe.

She pressed her hand to her chest and the breath she blew out left a white cloud in the air. Dad must not have turned the heat on yet. At least Cameron had picked a hiding spot that wasn't outside. Although she couldn't believe that he'd walked here on his own. It had to be over a mile from Asher's house to her parents' place.

"Cam?" Tugging off her boots, she left them beside his sneakers and padded into the great room.

White sheets spattered with beige paint were draped over her father's wooden sawhorses, creating a cave in the middle of the unfinished living area. She glimpsed a little boy's orange sock peeking out from under the sheets.

Biting back a smile, she crept forward, then sank to her knees on the laminate floor. "Hello?" She tapped the sheet with her finger, sending a ripple across the fabric. "Are there any dinosaur experts in this cave?"

Still no response.

"Cam, I'm here to help. If you'll come out, we can tackle whatever you're hiding from. Together."

She waited. The sound of fabric brushing against the floor made her breath hitch. Then he flipped back the sheet and scooted toward her on his bottom. Tears welled in his eyes. "Promise you'll help?"

"Oh, buddy." She spread her arms out and he fell against her. "Of course."

"Daddy's going to be so mad at me," he wailed. "I'm scared."

"It's okay to be scared." Patting the back of his jacket, she measured her words. "Why don't we walk over to my parents' house? I'll let your dad know you're safe."

"I don't want to go to the doctor."

"This person you're seeing isn't the kind of doctor who gives you shots or anything. She'll help you learn to be a better reader. That's all."

He pulled away, his dark eyelashes moist with tears. "I don't like reading," he whispered.

"I understand. Reading's important, though. We need to make sure you learn how." She pushed to her feet.

"Let's go see if my mother will fix you some hot cocoa while we wait for your dad to get here."

"Does she have marshmallows?"

She chuckled. "We can ask her."

He scooted back under the sheet, then popped back out holding a stuffed sea otter.

"Who's this?"

"Sammy the sea otter." Cameron hugged him tight. "He's my favorite."

She petted the sea otter's tummy. "Nice to meet you, Sammy."

Cameron held Sammy close to his ear, his eyebrows furrowed as he pretended to listen intently. Then he nodded. "Sammy says it's nice to meet you and he's glad you found us."

Was there anything more adorable than a kid with a vivid imagination? She playfully flipped his hoodie over his head. "I'm glad I found you, too."

Cameron squealed and shoved his hood back where it belonged as they walked toward the door.

He flopped on the floor and tugged his sneakers on. "I took my shoes off because I didn't want to get in trouble for getting the floors dirty."

Oh, he was so precious. She hated that something had scared him enough to make him run and hide. "That's very thoughtful. Thank you. Come on, let's go see about that hot chocolate."

Once they had their sneakers and boots on, Tess led the way outside. The rain had transitioned to huge snowflakes.

"It's snowing!" Cameron tipped his head back and stuck out his tongue. "Look, watch me catch one."

Tess reached out and ruffled his hair. "Very impressive."

As they jogged across the yard, Cameron slipped his hand into hers. She glanced down and grinned. When he smiled back, warmth unfurled in her chest. This kid. She wasn't supposed to have favorite students, but he'd claimed a spot in her top five.

They tromped up the steps and rushed inside. Eliana, Mrs. Lovell and Tess's mother stood in the entryway.

"Oh, Cameron, I'm so happy to see you." Mom pulled him in for a hug. "Are you all right?"

"Yep." Cameron tugged off his shoes. "Do you have any hot cocoa?"

"Absolutely." She herded Cameron toward the kitchen. "I'm so glad you're safe."

"Can we put marshmallows in my cocoa?"

"Of course."

"There's a box full of toy cars we can play with while we wait." Eliana trailed after them. "Does that sound fun?"

He hesitated. "Hot cocoa first, please."

Eliana and Mom's laughter filled the air.

Tess pulled her phone from her pocket. "I need to let Asher know Cameron's here, then I'll join you."

"Well, isn't this wonderful?" Mrs. Lovell clasped her hands under her chin. "Mother and son reunited."

Tess's scalp prickled. "What do you mean?"

Mrs. Lovell's complexion paled. "I—I thought you knew."

"Knew what?"

"Oh, honey, isn't it obvious? He looks just like you and your brother, Charlie." Mrs. Lovell pulled her keys from her parka. "I'd better let you sort this out."

"Wait. You can't—"

"I'll spread the word that the boy's been found." She waggled her fingers, then slipped out the front door. "Tell your mother I'll reach out about the furniture later."

Tess stared after her. *Mother and son reunited.*

Was it true? Or a cruel joke from a tactless woman?

Had she really spent hours with her own child and didn't know? Her head spun with the thought. How was that possible?

Fury rose inside her, like a storm rolling in off the Gulf of Alaska. Would Asher really deceive her like this? Ask her to babysit, let her tutor Cam and allow her to spend all this time with him and still not tell her the truth?

No matter who his mother was, that little boy deserved to learn how to read. Today was his opportunity to take the next step in the process. She wouldn't be responsible for making them miss their flight.

She typed out a text to Asher.

Please come to my parents' place ASAP.

Spots peppered her vision. It all made sense now— the way her heart went out to Cameron. The comments that he resembled Charlie. Even Ben had suspected a connection. And every time she saw Asher, he'd withheld the truth.

He'd tricked her.

With fingers trembling, she typed out the rest of the message: I found our son.

She hit Send, then sank onto the sofa, dropping her

phone in her lap. Cameron was the baby she thought she'd placed with an adoptive family. How could Asher do this?

"I found our son?"

Asher read the text message again. *Oh no. Oh no, no, no.*

"She knows."

"What's going on?" Mom sat in the passenger seat of his truck, her phone pressed to her ear. She'd already left a voice mail for Krista and now she had Justin on the line.

Asher's heart pounded and he stared at his phone. His whole body trembled. This couldn't be happening. "Tess knows." His voice didn't sound like his own. "I've got to get over there."

"Justin, I'll call you back." Mom ended the call. Her phone slipped from her hand and landed on the floorboards. "Son, you're not making sense. Did someone find Cameron?"

"Tess." Asher checked over his shoulder, then shifted into Reverse and backed out of his parking spot. "She sent a text that said she found *our* son."

"Oh, dear." Mom clasped her hand to her mouth.

He eased his truck out of the café's parking lot and onto the street, adrenaline pulsing through his veins. "That means she found out the truth from someone else. She's going to hate me. Cameron's going to hate me."

"You don't know that. Cameron is a very loving and kind little boy. What if he's delighted that Tess is his mother?"

"He won't be delighted when he figures out I've lied to him for seven years. I'm a horrible father."

"That is not true."

"Yes it is. What kind of dad deceives his own kid?" Asher tightened his grip on the steering wheel. "And Tess will never forgive me."

"That's a rather bold assumption on your part."

He fired a glare across the console.

"Forgiveness is a process." Mom's expression softened as her eyes filled with empathy. "It takes time. She has every right to be upset, but it's also possible that she won't carry a grudge forever. You have a child together. You're going to find a way through this."

Asher bit back another snarky response and focused on the road instead. Wet snowflakes dumped from a granite-gray sky, slowing traffic on Main Street. This wasn't the time to pour salt in his mother's wounds by reminding her that she ought to know grudges often jammed a wedge between people who'd once loved each other.

"Will you please use my phone and tell her we're on the way? And then text Brian. He's the one leading up the search from the community center. Tell him Cameron's fine."

"I'm on it."

"Thank you."

While he drove to the Maddens' house, his mother sent texts and called the church secretary to ask her to update their social media page. He was grateful. He wouldn't have thought to inform as many people that they had found Cameron. But as he pulled into the Maddens' driveway and saw Tess's car, his heart bottomed out. Maybe Mom should've asked the church to pray for him, because he had no idea how he was going to get through this conversation.

He grabbed the door handle.

"Wait."

He hesitated.

"We need to pray."

"Go ahead." Asher released his hold on the handle and bowed his head.

"Lord, thank You for loving us, even when we've made mistakes. Please help Asher and Tess. Give them courage for these tough conversations. And please protect Cameron. Remind him that we love him, and give us the grace for whatever comes next, Father. Amen."

Asher opened his eyes, but he couldn't move. Had that been his mother? He'd never heard her pray before. Well, maybe a time or two before they ate their Christmas and Thanksgiving meals.

But this prayer was different.

This was genuine authentic faith. He reached over and clasped her hand in his. "Thank you, Mom. That meant a lot to me."

Her eyes glistened with moisture. She offered a sad smile. "I'm sorry for everything I've done that brought you to this point. I can't help but wonder if things might've been different had I—"

"We all played a part in this. No matter what happens, I do not regret raising Cameron."

"I want to come with you. I want to apologize."

"Then let's go."

They climbed out of his truck. Asher hunched his shoulders against the dime-sized snowflakes landing on the bare skin at the nape of his neck. His gut churned with every step toward the Maddens' porch. He'd always imagined that once Tess discovered the truth, he'd feel so much better. So relieved. No more living a lie. Except bringing the truth into the light would hurt her.

And he dreaded telling Cameron that Tess was his mom. Sure, he might be thrilled. Might take it all in stride. But what if he didn't? What if it crushed him?

Or what if he blamed Asher for not telling him sooner?

Nothing tormented him more than the idea of hurting his little boy.

Before he could knock, the door opened, and Tess stood on the other side.

"Is it true?" Her eyes toggled between Asher and his mother. "Is Cameron my son?"

Blood roared in Asher's ears. "Yes."

She pressed her hands over her face. Tears streamed down her cheeks.

He should have told her the truth from the start. When she'd insisted on an adoption plan, he'd been within his rights to keep Cameron. But his father's plan had seemed easier. Why did he ever think Tess wouldn't find out?

Especially since they all lived in the same small town. Her shoulders trembled as she sobbed. Guilt and regret weighed heavy. He'd always hated to see her cry.

He exchanged worried glances with his mother. "Can we come in? I need to see Cameron and we need to talk."

Tess whirled away. She walked into the living room and sank onto the couch. He stepped inside. His mother followed and closed the door. "I'll check on Cameron," she whispered.

He nodded, then grabbed a box of tissues from the entryway table on his way into the living room. "Tess, it's going to be all right." He sank to his knees beside her. "We're going to figure this out. Together."

She reached up and pulled off her hat, then raked her fingers through her long hair. When her gaze met his, the hurt swimming in her eyes drove another spike of regret straight through his heart. "How could you, Asher?"

Chapter Twelve

She twisted her hat in her hands, squeezing the damp knit fabric to keep from hurling the box of tissues Asher offered across the room. "I need answers."

"You told me you didn't want to be a mother, but that doesn't mean I couldn't be a father."

"But you signed adoption papers." Her voice broke as she dropped her hat on the couch, then plucked the tissue box from his hands. "We agreed he'd be placed with a family off the island."

He rubbed the back of his neck. "There's more to that story—"

"Wait." She held up her palm. "Let me guess. That's how you pulled this off. The papers weren't real."

Asher shook his head slowly.

"And the woman—this person I assumed all along was Cameron's mother—this girlfriend that I believed you married in Oregon. She doesn't exist, does she?"

A muscle in his jaw tightened. "I wasn't dating anyone in Oregon, and I've never been married."

"So many lies." She mopped at her tears with the

tissue. "Who knew your family was capable of such diabolical behavior?"

"It's called *love*, Tess." The words came out rough. His voice gravelly. "I never wanted our child placed with an adoptive family. Yes, my father came up with the plan to use fraudulent papers, and that was wrong. But I went along with it because I looked at Cameron in the hospital nursery, and there was no way he was going home with anyone else except for me."

"But you tricked me." She pounded the arm of the sofa with her fist. "All this time I thought he was with a family. I thought he had a mom and a dad, a stable home and—"

"He has had a stable home. He's been with me, his father, for seven years. His aunt and uncle filled the gaps when I couldn't be with him. Please don't make this sound like I've caused some sort of irreparable harm to our son. You're the one who didn't want to be a parent."

His razor-sharp words sliced her heart. He'd gone too far. "You've been raising our son in secret and now you're blaming me? That's not fair. How about an apology? How about a plausible explanation?"

Asher groaned and tipped his head back. "Our deception snowballed into something much bigger than we ever expected. My mom created a salacious story to distract everyone from the truth. I wish she hadn't lied about a marriage that never happened. But here's the thing, and I know I have no right to ask you to believe me, but this is the truth. When I found out that letting another family adopt our baby boy meant I'd never see him again, and my parents told me there was a way that I could keep him, I wasn't going to let anything stand between me and my son. You made your choice, Tess, and I had to make mine."

Again with the blame. She looked away. The fire crackled and snapped, filling the silence. Unbelievable. Never in a million years did she suspect Asher and his parents would do something so horrible.

"Daddy? Miss Test?" Cameron peeked around the wall separating the kitchen from the living room. "Are you guys fighting about me?"

His question sent a chill racing through her, like she'd plunged into the ocean in the dead of winter.

"Sweet boy, come here." Tess sniffed and motioned for Cameron to join them. He inched closer. The fear in his eyes made her arms ache to pull him close.

"Hey, buddy." Asher reached for him. "I'm so glad you're okay."

Cameron sidestepped his embrace and climbed onto the couch beside her. Chocolate ringed his mouth. Tess smoothed his hair off his forehead. "Did you find some hot cocoa?"

He nodded, kicking his stocking feet against the couch. "Marshmallows, too."

Though her heart was breaking, she forced a smile. "Good for you."

Asher cleared his throat. "Miss Tess and I have something to tell you."

What? No. He wasn't going to tell him now, was he? She shook her head. "Asher, not yet."

"We can't wait any longer." Asher stood and skirted the coffee table, then sat down on Cameron's opposite side. "Cameron, I need you to listen closely. This is super important."

Another shiver racked her body. What if Cameron

flipped out? He and Asher still had a flight to catch and a crucial appointment this afternoon.

Cameron's eyes rounded. "'Kay."

"Once upon a time, Tess was my girlfriend and I loved her very much."

"Your girlfriend." Cameron tipped his head back and giggled. "No way."

That laugh buoyed her.

"I promise everything I'm about to tell you is true." Asher pressed his lips together. "Including the part that's going to hurt."

Cameron's laughter faded. "What's going to hurt?"

"I'd like to tell him." She rubbed her palm against Cameron's back. Adrenaline hummed in her veins. "When I was about nineteen, I grew a baby in my tummy. I loved that baby just like I loved your daddy."

He stared up at her, his expression so trusting she could barely squeeze the words past the emotion cresting inside. "Guess what? That baby is you. Cameron, I'm your mother."

His face lit up like sunshine bursting through storm clouds. The joy reflected in his eyes made her heart expand.

"Really?" he whispered.

She swiped at her tears with the back of her hand. "Really."

Cameron shifted toward Asher. "Is it true? Miss Test is my mom?"

"It's true." Asher's eyes deepened to a shade of velvety blue as he fought back tears.

Then Cameron flung his arms around Tess and buried his face in her jacket. She hugged him tight, not holding back. He smelled like chocolate and laundry soap and she never wanted to let go. Squeezing her eyes shut, she soaked in his unbridled affection.

He doesn't hate me.

"Wait a second." Cameron pulled back. That adorable crinkle marred his brow again. "How come you never told me?"

Oh, this was the question she'd dreaded. He was so young. Too young to fully comprehend the agony she'd endured.

Lord, give us the words, she silently pleaded.

It would be easy to pin the blame on Asher. His family's schemes had set this whole saga in motion. But if they had any hope of moving forward, she had to put her feelings into words without overwhelming Cameron.

"I wish I had told you sooner," Asher said. "I'm sorry that I waited so long. Here's what I want you to remember. Tess—your mom—and I love you very much. Your aunts, uncles and grandparents all love you, too. We did what we thought was best for you. Grown-ups don't always make the right choices and I am so sorry I kept the secret from you."

"It's okay, Daddy." Cameron spread his arms wide. "I still love you a whole bunch." Asher's face crumpled and he offered a wobbly smile. Tess clasped her palm over her mouth to hold back a sob. This boy was such a precious gift. And he was *hers*.

Cameron and Asher hugged. Asher's shoulders shook as he cried and whispered more apologies into Cameron's ear.

She retrieved the tissue box from the coffee table.

"I apologize for interrupting." Mrs. Hale spoke from the kitchen doorway. "Asher, I had your phone in my pocket and you just received an alert from the airlines. Your flight's delayed an hour."

Tess glanced at the clock mounted on the wall beside the fireplace. "If you go now you can still make it."

Asher shook his head, then swiped at his cheeks with his fingers. "We can reschedule."

"No, this appointment is important," Tess said. "You need to go."

"I want to stay here." Cameron looped his arm through hers. "I don't want to go to my 'pointment."

She was torn. Selfishly, she didn't want to let him out of her sight. They had so much lost time to make up for. But he needed this intervention more. She pressed a kiss to his hair. "Remember what we talked about when I found you earlier? This appointment will be different?"

Cameron frowned. "Yes."

"Everything I said to you is still true. Reading is important. Your dad and I want to make sure you learn to read, and this appointment today will help. I promise."

"Fine." Cameron flopped back against the couch with a dramatic sigh that would rival any teenager's efforts. "I'll go."

"Did you want to…"

Asher trailed off before he completed the question. Her insides quaked. "No, I— That's not a good idea."

She wasn't ready for a weekend trip off the island, just the three of them. Not yet. Maybe never. Asher had betrayed her. They couldn't possibly pretend everything was fine.

Confusion filled Asher's expression. *But this is your son. Don't you want to be involved?*

"I'll be here when you get back." She quickly addressed his unspoken questions. "You probably still have some packing to do."

"Are you sure?" Asher pushed to his feet. "I can call and see if there are any seats available on the plane?"

She stood and walked toward the door. "Come on, Cam. I'll help you with your shoes."

Cameron trailed after her and flopped on the floor. "I can't believe you're my mom," he whispered, shoving his foot into his sneaker.

Me, either.

"What a fun surprise, right?" She helped him double-knot his shoestrings. "I'll be praying for you and I can't wait to hear all about your trip."

Asher helped Cameron put on his jacket while Mom, Eliana and Mrs. Hale joined them.

"We'd better go." Mrs. Hale slipped past Tess and opened the door. Outside, she hesitated on the porch and turned back.

Tess shivered against the cold air swirling around her and braced for impact. The woman wasn't known for her grace and tact. Mrs. Hale opened her mouth, then clamped it shut, offering only an apologetic glance instead.

Probably for the best. Tess had so much she wanted to say right now, but feared she'd only regret whatever words came out.

Cameron flung his arms around her waist. Her throat tightened against another swell of emotion. *Don't. Don't fall apart now.*

She leaned down and kissed the top of his head. "Be brave."

"I will." He pulled away, then trotted after his grand-mother, tugging his hood over his head. A soft blanket of snow coated the yard and vehicles. Cameron scooped a pile of snow from the porch railing, formed a ball, then flung it at a tree.

"Nailed it!" He whooped with delight, turning around and flashing them an adorable grin. Tess offered a thumbs-up, smiling through her tears.

Asher lingered, twisting his key chain around his finger.

She wrapped her arms around her torso and met his gaze. *Please, just go.*

"I'm sorry."

The sorrow swimming in his eyes nearly split her heart in two.

"Thank you." Two simple words were all she could manage. He slipped outside, closing the door softly behind him. Another sob spilled from her lips, then she fell apart in her mother's arms.

Ten miserable hours later, Asher sat in a hotel room in Anchorage, a half-eaten deli sandwich on the desk in front of him. Cam had fallen asleep on the sofa. They'd picked a college basketball game to watch on television, but Asher didn't have the energy to focus.

He scrubbed his hand over his face. Every muscle in his body ached from fatigue. From the adrenaline-fueled search for Cameron, to the emotional conversation with Tess, plus the whirlwind trip to Anchorage and a grueling appointment, he hadn't had more than a couple of minutes to himself all day.

A knock at the door tugged him back to reality. He padded across the thick carpet, then peered through the peephole. His brother, Justin, stood in the hallway. Asher turned the dead bolt and tugged open the door.

"What are you doing here?"

"Surprise." Justin grinned. "Good to see you, big brother."

Asher leaned against the doorframe. "I didn't know you were in town this weekend."

"Kind of a last-minute thing." Justin craned his neck to see into the room. "Is Cameron awake? I'd like to say hello."

Asher moved back and motioned for Justin to come in.

Justin stepped inside, towing his rolling suitcase behind him.

"Uncle Justin?" Cameron sat up and rubbed his eyes. "What are you doing here?"

"Hey, little dude." Justin unzipped his black jacket and slung it over the back of Asher's chair. "I came to see you."

"Yay." Cameron hopped off the sofa, his hair sticking up as he scampered into Justin's waiting arms.

Justin chuckled and swung Cam into the air, then turned him upside down. Cameron giggled.

"Take it easy, Justin. Unless you want to see his sub sandwich again." Asher did not want to clean up that kind of mess.

"That's a negative." Justin carefully set Cameron on his feet. "What are you guys up to tonight?"

"Nothing." Cameron pooched out his lower lip. "Dad said we had to stay here and relax."

"Well, that's no fun." Justin glanced at Asher. "Rough day?"

"Yep." Asher wrapped up his sandwich and tucked it into the mini-fridge. Mom might've filled Justin in on everything that had gone down in Hearts Bay this morning, but he wasn't sure. And he didn't want to re-hash it all now.

His phone hummed with an incoming text.

"Is that Tess?" Cameron craned his neck to see the phone's screen.

"Doubt it." Asher grabbed the phone from the desk. "She's pretty upset."

"She's not upset at me."

"You're right. She's not." Because this disaster was all his doing. Guilt pinched Asher's insides. Way to go. Father of the year.

He'd mentally replayed their conversation in her parents' house during the flight from Orca Island to Anchorage. Well, when Cameron wasn't peppering him with questions. Tess's words had cut deep. He'd wanted to defend himself. He'd wanted to remind her that she'd broken his heart. More than anything, he'd wanted her to understand that everything he'd done, he'd done because he loved her and their baby.

But none of that mattered now.

"Cameron, it's time to put on your pajamas." Asher reached inside the duffel bag slouching on the floor at his feet. He pulled out the clothes and handed them to Cameron. "Why don't you get ready for bed while me and Uncle Justin catch up."

"Okay."

No argument. Wow, he must really be tired.

Cameron clutched his pajamas to his chest and headed for the bathroom. "If I get ready fast, can we call my mom?"

His question landed like a gut punch. It wasn't one he'd been prepared for. "Of course."

Once the door was closed, Asher faced his brother.

"His mom?" Justin's eyebrows sailed upward. "What's that about?"

Asher checked to make sure Cameron had closed the bathroom door, then sank down on the bed closest to the couch.

"Cameron's been having trouble with reading and we found out today that he's dyslexic."

"Oh, wow." Justin frowned. "Sorry to hear that."

"Yeah, me, too." The diagnosis wasn't a complete surprise. Part of him had clung to the hope that maybe there was a simple solution to solve Cameron's struggles. Mrs. Bridger had offered encouragement and outlined next steps, but the weight of the added responsibility overwhelmed him. Worse, he did not know how to move forward without Tess's guidance.

"Tess Madden is teaching at Cameron's school and they also hired her to work with kids who struggle with reading."

Justin took a seat on the couch. "Like a tutor?"

Asher nodded. "She's been working with Cam after school for several weeks, but he made little progress. We came here to see a child psychologist for an intervention. Anyway, long story short, Tess and Cam got super attached and someone informed her this morning that she's his mother."

Justin released a low whistle. "He finds out his tutor is really his mother and he's dyslexic all in the same day? That's a lot for one kid to handle."

"It's a lot for this grown-up to handle."

Justin braced his ankle on his knee and slung his arm over the back of the couch. "How'd Tess take the news?"

"Not great. We didn't have time to talk because Cameron and I had to catch our flight. She's upset."

"Have you tried groveling?"

"You're hilarious."

"I wasn't joking," Justin said. "Are you planning on joint custody?"

"I was hoping more like a do-over. A restart on our relationship."

"That's a good plan."

"Or the dumbest idea ever."

"Do you love her?"

"Never stopped."

"Not that you asked, but my advice would be to get on the next plane back to the island and tell her how you feel."

"Yeah, right. If only it were that easy. I sent her a text as soon as our appointment was over and shared Cameron's diagnosis. Then I offered to answer any questions she had, trying to include her, you know? But the only thing she bothered to text back was that she was thankful for a definitive answer and she appreciated the news."

"Finding out her ex-boyfriend's been raising her kid in secret for seven years gave her a lot to think about."

He couldn't argue with that. And he kind of hated that Justin was offering excellent advice.

"Listen. Take it from a guy who's had to grovel a time or three. You'd be surprised what a genuine apology can do."

"Is that why you're here?"

Justin looked away, smoothing his palm across the top of his close-cropped hair. "I know I haven't been the most reliable brother."

He met Asher's gaze. The guilt reflected there softened Asher's defenses.

"To tell you the truth, after Mom and Dad's relationship turned so bitter and they divorced, I wanted nothing to do with family for a while."

"Ouch."

"Yeah, I know. I'm sorry. That's a lousy way to deal." Justin's expression brightened. "But I'm here and I want to do better. I will be better."

"That's good to hear."

"When Mom called and told me Cameron was missing, I felt terrible. You didn't need another thing on top of all the other stuff you're already dealing with, so I cleared my schedule and flew in to help."

"Help with…Mom? Cameron? What's your plan, Justin?"

The bathroom door flew open and Cameron bounded out. "Okay, I'm ready. Let's call my mom."

Justin grinned. "I'm here to kick-start Operation Win Tess's Heart."

"Perfect." Asher smiled and held out his fist. "I need all the help I can get. When do we begin?"

Justin bumped Asher's fist with his. "Stick with me, bro. I got this."

Tess stared through the living window at the overcast sky and fresh snow coating her car. Spending the rest of fall break in Hawaii sounded amazing. If she packed now and caught the next flight to Anchorage, she could be in Honolulu by late tonight.

A tempting notion. Except her rational side knew lounging on the beach in a tropical paradise wouldn't provide an escape from the heartache. And she had to be here for Cameron when he came home.

Cameron. Her son. When Asher let him use Face-

Time to call her on Friday, she'd longed to leap through the screen and hug her precious boy. She'd tried to tell him that dyslexia wasn't the end of the world. And that she had all kinds of strategies to make reading possible. Maybe even fun.

But all he'd wanted to talk about was the toys Mrs. Bridger had in her office, the equipment on the airport runway that deiced the plane's wings, and how happy he was to see Uncle Justin.

She'd stayed strong the whole time. Forced a bright smile and said all the right things. After they ended the call, she'd buried her head in her hands and sobbed. Again.

Oh, she was so tired of crying.

But everything about this situation terrified her. What if Cameron rejected her? When he got older, what if he put the missing pieces together and accused her of abandonment? How would he ever trust another adult again?

"Here." Eliana held out a plate of toast buttered with a dollop of Grandmother's raspberry jam. She set a mug of steaming coffee on the coaster in the middle of the coffee table. "You've got to eat something."

"I'm not hungry," Tess whispered.

"That's what you've been saying for two days straight. I can't imagine how you're feeling but starving yourself will not help. You're Cameron's mother. Soon he's going to need you and you're going to need your strength."

Tess grabbed the throw pillow and hugged it to her chest. "I still can't believe it. How am I supposed to move forward?"

Sure, she'd prayed about it, and deep down she trusted

that the Lord was with them, even in the midst of their mistakes. But she still wrestled with guilt. Shame, too. She'd done what she'd thought was best for her baby. Given the opportunity to do it all over, she'd still choose to make an adoption plan. No matter how much support their families might've offered, in her heart of hearts, she knew she wasn't ready to be a mother at nineteen. Her education and her teaching certification gave her a stable job with benefits. And she wouldn't trade her experience teaching school in Fairbanks for anything.

Well, almost anything. Knowing that Asher had parented Cameron alone for the past seven years had ramped up her guilt. She'd missed so much. First smile, first words, first steps…first everything.

"You and Asher are going to figure this out." Eliana squeezed her arm. "Who knows? Maybe this revelation will be the catalyst that brings you back together."

"That's what I'm afraid of." He'd just admitted to raising their child in secret. She was supposed to be livid.

Right?

"I think it's normal to feel apprehensive," Eliana said. "Please try to remember that God is not surprised by any of this. He will equip you for whatever comes next."

Tess knew Eliana was right. God was well aware of all the choices she and Asher and his parents had made. Yet He'd graciously reunited her with her son. And with Asher, too. Now that she'd spent time with him and with Cameron, and observed Asher's parenting skills, she was beginning to understand why he hadn't been able to follow through with the adoption. Leaping back into a romantic relationship was still terrifying, though. After all, they weren't the same people they were seven years ago. What if she and Asher started over, tried dating again, only to discover they weren't meant to be?

Cameron would be crushed.

"Why am I even thinking about this?" She tossed the pillow aside and reached for the coffee. "Asher and I have way too much history between us."

"Way too much history to not try again. That's what you meant to say, right?" Eliana winked, then twisted her hair into a bun. "I need to go to the café. Kelly's kids are sick, so there's no one else to supervise the morning shift. Are you sure you're going to be all right if I leave you alone? Mom said she can come by after church if you need company."

"I'm fine." To prove her point, she grabbed the toast and nibbled on a corner. She should go to church, but she couldn't face the stares or the relentless questions. And she wasn't ready to see Asher's mother yet.

"I'll check in later and see how you're doing. Love you." Eliana's keys jangled as she pulled them from the hook by the door. "Text if you need anything."

"Love you, too."

Eliana left. Except Tess couldn't stop rehashing their conversation. Giving Asher another chance was out of the question.

Wasn't it?

Although she had to admit, since they'd both moved back to the island, his presence in her life had reignited old feelings. But as soon as she embraced the idea, a fresh wave of hurt rolled in. Tess sipped her coffee, quickly realizing that she didn't want to be alone. The hum of the dishwasher wasn't much company. Burrowing under the blanket, she dug the remote out from between the cushions, then clicked on the television and surfed through the channels. There had to be a favorite rom-com streaming somewhere. She'd get lost in a movie like she'd always done when she wanted to escape.

Three minutes into *The Wedding Planner*, someone knocked on the door.

Drat. She glanced down at her flannel pajamas layered under a comfy robe. The same thing she'd been wearing since Friday afternoon.

She slid lower on the couch, protecting her coffee from spilling, and clicked the remote to mute the volume. Maybe they'd go away. She hadn't showered in three days. Or bothered to do much with her hair. She wasn't in the mood for visitors.

They knocked again, louder this time. Heaving a sigh, she flung the blanket aside and set her coffee down. She grabbed an elastic hair band lying on the coffee table and tugged her hair into a ponytail as she walked to the door.

Peeking out the window, she sucked in her breath at the sight of Cameron and Asher standing outside.

Cameron held an enormous bouquet. Asher stood behind him with a box of chocolates and a stack of what she assumed were books wrapped in brown paper and tied together with twine.

Oh, how sweet.

Yanking open the door, she couldn't stop a smile. "What are you guys doing here?"

"Cameron has a few birthdays, Christmases and Mother's Days to make up for." Asher offered a hesitant smile. "We thought we'd try to catch up."

"But this is all I could carry." Cameron grunted and

thrust the bouquet of pink, white and red roses into her arms. "Here. Can you hold these, please?"

"Of course." She cradled the bouquet in the crook of her elbow, then knelt and pulled him in with her other arm. "I've missed you."

"It's only been a few days." Cameron squirmed in her embrace. "Why are you still in your jammies?"

"Because I wasn't expecting company." She stood and moved out of the way. "Would you like to come in?"

"Yep." Cameron squeezed past her. "Do you have any toys here?"

"There's a bin of Lego sets beside the TV stand." She'd snagged Charlie's old collection from her parents' house to take back to her classroom. "Why don't you see what you can build?"

Asher moved closer and held out the books and chocolate. "These are for you. Cam thought you needed chocolate, and the manager at the bookstore in Anchorage said these were the hottest new releases."

"Thank you." She stepped inside and closed the door behind him. "That was very thoughtful."

She set all the gifts on the dining room table, then faced him. His blue eyes roamed her face. She couldn't look away.

"I am so sorry," Asher said. "I know there's nothing I can do or say to make up for all the deception. I hope with time you can forgive me and make space in your life for Cameron."

"And what about you?"

His brow crimped. "What about me?"

"Can I make space in my life for you, too?"

He swallowed hard. "I thought that was too much to hope for. What are you saying?"

"I'm saying that I'm terrified. I'm saying I want to forgive you, but I'm still so hurt."

Confusion flashed in his eyes. "That doesn't sound like you want me in your life. Quite the opposite, actually."

Ugh. This was hard. Much harder than she'd anticipated. She fisted her hands in the pockets of her robe and drew a wobbly breath. "Letting you back in as anything more than a co-parent means I have to be vulnerable. That scares me, Asher."

His features softened. "I'm scared, too."

"I'm worried if I refuse to trust that God has something wonderful in mind for all three of us, then that might mean I miss out on the blessing of being part of an amazing family." Hot tears pressed against the backs of her eyes. "And I'm afraid I'll regret that forever."

Asher looked away. He ran his fingers along his jaw. Was he struggling to control his emotions, too? Did her words even make sense?

"We've both wrestled with guilt and regret. For far too long." His voice was thick with emotion as his gaze locked on hers. "I don't want us to live like that. I don't believe God wants us to live that way, either."

Her heart hammered against her ribs. Was she a fool for seriously considering giving their relationship a fresh start?

"Forgiveness is a process and a choice. Take all the time you need. Even though I don't deserve a second chance, I desperately want one."

His tender revelation softened the last of her resistance.

"Then let's try again." The words tumbled from her lips. She didn't want to snatch them back, though. This time they felt right. They felt good. She slid her palms along Asher's jacket sleeves, then tipped her chin up.

Asher cupped her face in his hands. "You have no idea how badly I wanted to hear you say that."

"I'm still really scared," she whispered. "But I want to be brave. For Cameron and for us."

His minty breath feathered her skin as he angled his head. The pads of his thumbs caressed her cheekbones. She leaned into his touch and closed her eyes.

He brushed her lips with his own. A gentle whisper of a kiss.

"Ew, gross." Cameron's declaration drew a rumble from Asher's chest.

She smiled against Asher's lips.

He touched his forehead to hers. "I love you, Tess Madden. I never stopped loving you."

"I love you, too."

He kissed her again as Cameron dumped the entire bin of plastic bricks onto the floor. She didn't even flinch. Something told her this moment offered a glimpse of her future. This time she wouldn't run. They'd embrace the beautiful and the messy parts of life. Together.

Epilogue

The diamond ring was burning a hole in his pocket.

"Guys, watch me," Cameron yelled.

Oh no. Those three words often preceded a questionable choice. Asher opened his mouth to issue a warning, but the words died on his lips as Cameron turned a cartwheel on the grass in front of the Maddens' house.

Asher stared. When did he learn to do that?

Cameron landed on his feet and flashed a proud grin.

"Impressive." Tess clapped, then smiled at Asher. Her bright eyes and wide smile reflected her pride. "I taught him that."

Asher chuckled. "Of course you did." He pulled her close, planting a quick kiss on her hair. The familiar citrus fragrance of her shampoo teased his senses. She looped her arm around his waist and leaned against him. He caressed her shoulder and silently willed his brother to hurry up and take the photo.

"Almost ready." Justin stood nearby, fiddling with his camera on the tripod. "Cam, it's picture time. Go stand by your parents."

Asher, Tess, Grandmother Madden, and Tess's parents and sisters had gathered to celebrate Mother's Day and Cameron's eighth birthday. Only Justin and Eliana knew of Asher's intentions to propose.

"Here I come." Cameron tugged the hem of his rumpled camouflage-print T-shirt down and ran toward Tess. Asher winced at the grass stain on Cameron's khaki cargo pants. Oh, well. At least his face didn't have chocolate on it and he'd combed his hair.

"That was an epic cartwheel." Tess guided him into position beside her. "Stand here beside Grandmother and give Uncle Justin your best smile."

"Then can I show you my somersault on the trampoline?" Cameron grinned at them, his eyes hopeful. Man, he looked so much like Tess.

"Absolutely." Tess patted his shoulder. "Can't wait."

Warmth flooded Asher's chest. These last seven months since Tess found out she was Cameron's mother had been incredible. Sure, they'd hit some snags. Conflicting opinions about parenting and coaching Cameron through his ongoing struggles with dyslexia had challenged their fragile relationship. But they'd also shared tender moments, plenty of kisses and a renewed commitment to building a life together. His mother was right. Forgiveness takes time. And Tess had taught him that it was also a choice. He would always be grateful that the Lord had worked in their hearts and helped them to choose love instead of bitterness.

"You are a busy fella." Grandmother patted Cameron's arm. "I wish I had half your energy."

"I'll share if you want, Grandmother." Cameron's comment sent a ripple of laughter through the Madden family.

"On three, everybody say 'cheese!'" Justin held

up three fingers from behind the camera. "One, two, three."

"Cheese!"

The camera's shutter clicked, while Asher's stomach did its own rendition of cartwheels and somersaults. The anticipation had kept him wound tight. He wasn't about to thwart Grandmother Madden's request for a family photo, but he couldn't let another hour go by without asking Tess to marry him.

Justin took the camera off the tripod and strode toward them. "Do you want to make sure I took one that you like?"

"No," Cameron and Asher protested in unison, earning an amused glance from Tess's mother.

"Come on, Mom." Cameron grabbed Tess's hand. "Let's jump on the trampoline."

Yikes. He'd asked Cameron's opinion about marrying Tess. The kid had zero objections. No surprise there. But Asher hadn't shared specific details about the proposal because he feared Cam might spoil the surprise.

He launched a pointed glance in Eliana's direction.

Her mouth twitched with a knowing smile. "Hey, buddy. I'll take you." Eliana tapped Cameron on the shoulder. "Tag, you're it. Last one to the trampoline is a rotten egg."

"Hey!" Cameron squealed, then raced after her.

"Let's take a walk." Asher laced his fingers through Tess's and tugged her away from the family, still gathered on the lawn.

"I'll never get tired of him calling me Mom," she said as they walked toward the rocky shoreline. "I'm proud of him. He's handled all of this upheaval in his life so well."

"That's because he has an amazing mother." Asher lifted their joined hands to his lips and brushed her knuckles with a kiss.

Pink blossomed on her cheeks. "You deserve credit, too. You're an incredible father."

He couldn't have asked for a more perfect day to propose. With the May sunshine warming their skin, they'd gathered with family to celebrate motherhood and Cameron's birthday. Now they stood together on the edge of the island infused with countless memories.

Asher stopped walking and faced her. His mouth turned to cotton. Legs wobbling, he pulled the ring box from his pocket and dropped to one knee. "Tess, you captured my heart when we were kids throwing stones in the water and building driftwood forts. You are the only one for me. It took time for us to find our way back to one another, but I'm thankful we came home because the past seven months have shown me that I am a better man and a better father when I have you by my side."

His hands shook as he flipped open the velvet box. "Tess Madden, will you marry me?"

Tears clung to her dark lashes. She tented her palms over her nose, then nodded quickly.

His heart soared and he jumped to his feet and swept her into his arms.

"Yes, yes, I will marry you, Asher Hale," she murmured into his neck.

Those were the sweetest words he'd ever heard. He slipped the diamond solitaire onto her ring finger, then whirled her around in a circle, savoring the warmth of her arms twined around him. The water lapping at the shoreline mingled with their laughter. She'd said yes.

Thank You, Lord.

He set her down, then framed her face with his hands. "I love you."

"I love you, too." Her golden-brown eyes searched his as she encircled his wrists with her hands. "I can't wait to be your wife."

He leaned down and kissed her. She responded, sliding her palms up over his shoulders as he deepened the kiss. Her touch, the breeze blowing her hair around them, the warmth of her arms linked around his neck all hinted at the wonderful future waiting for them.

Reluctantly, he pulled away and rested his forehead against hers. "How quickly can you plan a wedding?"

Her eyes sparkled. "How soon can we elope?"

Her question made his pulse stutter. "Seriously?"

"I wouldn't joke about that."

He kissed her again, a tender declaration that signaled his approval. "Is Memorial Day weekend too soon?"

"I'll start packing when I get home." She grinned that heart-stopping smile and slipped her hand into his. "Let's go tell Cameron."

They returned to the house and found everyone in the backyard. Conversation came to a halt when he and Tess strode toward the trampoline, where Eliana and Cameron bounced together.

Asher cupped his hands around his mouth. "Hey, everyone, we have an announcement."

"We're getting married." Tess held up her hand. The diamond engagement ring sparkled in the sunlight.

Cheers and applause rang out.

Cameron came to the edge of the trampoline and poked his head through the opening in the safety net. "Is that true?"

"Absolutely." Tess smiled at their son. "Our fun facts are always true."

Cameron's eyes lit up. "So we'll be together always and forever?"

Tess's beautiful eyes found his. "Always and forever."

* * * * *

*Look for the next book in Heidi McCahan's
Home to Hearts Bay miniseries,
coming soon from Love Inspired!*

Dear Reader,

Have you ever thought about how your hometown has shaped your life? My family moved to Alaska when I was a baby, and I moved away when I went to college in Washington. I didn't fully appreciate my unique childhood until I started writing novels as an adult. Now I view my past experiences as a well of endless inspiration, and I'm grateful for the opportunity to pour my affection for Alaska into this new miniseries.

Much like Asher and Tess, my life choices have carried me far from the place I once called home. I don't get to go back and visit very often, but the positive influence of the people who shaped me—taught me to read, encouraged me to never stop learning and to strive for excellence—is reflected in the stories I write.

I hope you enjoyed your visit to Hearts Bay, and I look forward to sharing Eliana and Tate's story with you soon.

Thank you for supporting Christian fiction and telling your friends how much you enjoy our books. I'd love to connect with you. You can find me online: www.facebook.com/heidimccahan/, www.heidimccahan.com/ or www.instagram.com/heidimccahan.author. For news about book releases and sales, sign up for my author newsletter: www.subscribepage.com/heidimccahan-newoptin.

Until next time,
Heidi

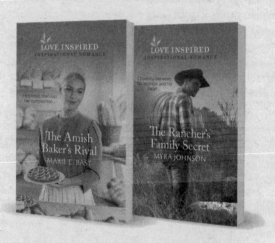

COMING NEXT MONTH FROM
Love Inspired

THE AMISH TWINS NEXT DOOR
Indiana Amish Brides • by Vannetta Chapman
Amish single mom Deborah Mast is determined to raise her seven-year-old twin sons *her* way. But when neighbor Nicholas Stoltzfus takes on the rambunctious boys as apprentices on his farm, she'll learn the value of his help with more than just the children—including how to reopen her heart.

SECRETS IN AN AMISH GARDEN
Amish Seasons • by Lenora Worth
When garden nursery owner Rebecca Eicher hires a new employee, she can't help but notice that Jebediah Martin looks similar to her late fiancé. But when her brother plays matchmaker, Jeb's secret is on the brink of being revealed. Will the truth bring them together or break them apart forever?

EARNING HER TRUST
K-9 Companions • by Brenda Minton
With the help of her service dog, Zeb, Emery Guthrie is finally living a life free from her childhood trauma. Then her high school bully, Beau Wilde, returns to town to care for his best friend's orphaned daughters. Has she healed enough to truly forgive him and let him into her life?

THEIR ALASKAN PAST
Home to Owl Creek • by Belle Calhoune
Opening a dog rescue in Owl Creek, Alaska, is a dream come true for veterinarian Maya Roberts, but the only person she can get to help her run it is her ex-boyfriend Ace Reynolds. When a financial situation forces Ace to accept the position, Maya can't run from her feelings...or the secret of why she ended things.

A NEED TO PROTECT
Widow's Peak Creek • by Susanne Dietze
Dairy shepherdess Clementine Simon's only concern is the safety of her orphaned niece and nephew and *not* the return of her former love Liam Murphy. But could the adventuring globe-trotter be just what she needs to overcome her fears and take another chance on love?

A PROMISE FOR HIS DAUGHTER
by Danielle Thorne
After arriving in Kudzu Creek, contractor and historical preservationist Bradley Ainsworth discovers the two-year-old daughter he never knew about living there with her foster mom, Claire Woodbury. But as they work together updating the house Claire owns, he might find the family he didn't know he was missing...

LOOK FOR THESE AND OTHER LOVE INSPIRED BOOKS WHEREVER BOOKS ARE SOLD, INCLUDING MOST BOOKSTORES, SUPERMARKETS, DISCOUNT STORES AND DRUGSTORES.

LICNM0322

SPECIAL EXCERPT FROM

LOVE INSPIRED
INSPIRATIONAL ROMANCE

With the help of her service dog, she's finally living her life, but is she healed enough to help her past bully care for two orphaned little girls?

Read on for a sneak preview of
Earning Her Trust *by Brenda Minton*
available May 2022 from Love Inspired.

The brick building that housed the county Division of Family Services always brought back a myriad of emotions for Emery Guthrie. As she stood on the sidewalk on a too-warm day in May, the memories came back stronger than ever.

Absently, she reached to pet her service dog, Zeb. The chocolate-brown labradoodle understood that touch and he moved close to her side. He grounded her to reality, to the present. She'd been rescued.

Rescued. She drew on that word. She'd been rescued. By this place, this building and the people inside. They'd seen her father jailed for the abuse that had left her physically and emotionally broken. They'd placed her with a foster mother, Nan Guthrie, the woman who had adopted her as a teen, giving her a new last name and a new life.

But today wasn't about Emery. It was about the two young girls whom Nan had been caring for the past few weeks. They'd lost their parents in a terrible, violent tragedy. They'd been uprooted from their home, their lives and all they'd ever known, brought to Pleasant, Missouri, and placed with Nan until their new guardian could be found.

That man was Beau Wilde. A grade ahead of Emery, Beau had spent their school years making her life even more miserable with his bullying.

He'd taunted, teased and humiliated her.

She shook her head, as if freeing herself from the thoughts she'd not allowed to see the light of day in many years. Those memories belonged in the past.

Just then, a truck pulled off the road and circled the parking lot.

Emery hesitated a moment too long. Beau was out of his truck and heading in her direction. He nodded as he closed in on her.

"Please, let me." He opened the door and stepped back to allow her to go first. "Nice dog."

"Thank you," she whispered. She cleared her throat. "His name is Zeb."

Don't miss
Earning Her Trust *by Brenda Minton*
wherever Love Inspired books and ebooks are sold.

LoveInspired.com

LIEXP0322